The Compromise

By Jo Maseberg

Copyright © 2003 by Jo Maseberg

All rights reserved.
No part of this book may be used or reproduced
in any manner whatsoever without written permission
except in the case of brief quotations
embodied in critical articles and reviews.

This is a fictional story.

A Fireside Library Book
OGDEN PUBLICATIONS INC.
Topeka, Kansas

Published by Ogden Publications
1503 S.W. 42nd St., Topeka, Kansas 66609

For more information about
Ogden Publications titles,
or to place an order, call:
(Toll-free) 1-800-678-4884.

ISBN 0-941678-72-5
First printing January 2003
Printed and bound
in the United States of America

To all of the students and teachers of the one-room country schools. The schools are nearly gone now, but the memories remain. Let's keep them alive as long as we can.

– Jo Maseberg

Chapter 1

The eastern Kansas weather was unusually mild for December, and with the temperature above sixty degrees, Ellie MacCready had the car windows rolled down and the Christmas carols on the radio turned up. As of this morning, she was officially on Christmas vacation – officially ready to buy Christmas gifts, she thought, as she downshifted and came to a stop at a busy intersection. She wasn't the only one it seemed. Everyone in Kansas City was out enjoying the nice weather, and everyone was Christmas shopping.

Three hours and a mere two gifts later, Ellie waded through the food court in the mall with a sandwich and a soda. An empty table stood near the far edge, and she wanted nothing more than to sit down and enjoy her lunch. Completely focused on her goal, she failed to notice a tall, blond woman waving at her from a nearby table.

"Ellie! Ellie MacCready! Over here!"

At the sound of her name, Ellie turned, spotting her friend a moment later.

The Compromise

"Jill!"

Ellie shifted direction and made for Jill's table, narrowly escaping a serious spill in the jostling crowd of hungry shoppers. As she placed her food and packages down and took a seat, she breathed a sigh of relief. Jill grinned and shook her head.

"Come now, at least you don't have to shop in the toy stores. You should see the mess. I nearly got trampled in one aisle and came close to starting a brawl in another."

"I just don't believe that of you, Jill. You're always so calm." Ellie took a bite of her sandwich as Jill shook her head.

"I'm a new woman, Ellie."

Ellie couldn't help but laugh at Jill's sorrowful expression and thought she'd never met a better doctor or a better friend.

"So ... " Jill changed the subject abruptly. "What are you doing for Christmas?"

"Well, I just finished teaching a special one-semester, grant-funded class, so I'm jobless. If I felt really motivated, I'd get on a plane and go to California. Mom and Dad are there spending Christmas with Robert and his family. Mark is celebrating the holiday with his new in-laws, and James is going to Aspen to stay with friends."

"That still doesn't tell me what you're doing."

"I just don't know."

Jill looked thoughtful for a moment, then brightened.

"Well, if you don't have plans, how about coming with us? Brian and I are taking the kids to Nebraska to spend Christmas with Mike and Jenny. How long has it been since you've been back to the hills?"

Ellie thought back to the last time that she'd seen the land where she grew up. She had been seventeen, and it had rained the day they left Nebraska. She hadn't been back since. "It's been a long time, Jill."

"Well, what do you say?"

"Are you sure Mike and Jenny won't mind?"

Jill laughed. "What's one extra mouth and one extra set of helping hands? Besides, you're an elementary teacher, and all our kids are that age. We can put you in charge of keeping them out of trouble. You must know some good games."

"Oh, I see," Ellie said with a raise of her eyebrows. "Now I'm just a glorified baby sitter."

"Yup. So, how about it?"

Spending the holidays in the hills with her childhood friends and their children sounded like heaven to Ellie. Even the thought of the long drive in a crowded van with two little girls didn't put her off. She grinned at Jill and said, "Where do I sign up, and what do I bring?"

A week later, Ellie was belted into one of the seats in Brian and Jill's minivan; her luggage and gifts were in the back with everyone else's. They left Kansas City and

The Compromise

headed west. Emily, seven, and Beth, four, had joined the adults in singing Christmas carols and playing guessing games. Everyone had been surprised when noon came, and now, after eating and running around the parking lot, the two girls were dozing in their seats. Jill, too, was asleep. Even Brian was getting drowsy.

"Do you want me to drive for a while?" Ellie asked from her seat behind the driver. Brian looked up, and his eyes met hers in the mirror.

"Do you really want to?"

"Sure. I'm actually wide-awake. It must have been all the caffeine at lunch."

"That would be great."

Minutes later, Brian pulled into a rest stop, and they switched places. Ellie got back on the interstate, and within five minutes, Brian was asleep. She had a feeling that while both Brian and Jill loved being doctors, their hectic schedules were almost too much sometimes. Her own life was crazy, too, but she was so excited about going home that she couldn't sleep if she tried.

Going home. The words brought back all the old feelings – all the feelings she had pushed aside eleven years ago. As she drove west, she let her mind drift back, and she wondered if she had ever really gotten over losing the ranch.

A day later, as Jill drove off the highway onto the oil road leading to the Sand Hills, Ellie knew that she never had.

Jo Maseberg

The oil road turned to gravel ten miles later. The brown, rolling hills seemed stark and cold beneath the overcast sky; the cattle in the pastures gathered to eat hay.

"What are you thinking, Ellie?" Jill asked, glancing at Ellie in the passenger seat.

"Just feeling a little homesick," Ellie said, her eyes never leaving the hills and barbed wire fence along the road.

Brian and the girls were playing a guessing game, and the two women were able to tune them out.

"Leaving was harder on you than we ever realized, wasn't it?" Jill stopped and waited for a cow to get off the road, then drove on.

"I spent seventeen years on that ranch. If you wanted me to, I could sit down and draw a map of every pasture, every gate, every building and every windmill. When Mom and Dad had to sell, I was devastated. My brothers were away at college, so it didn't hit them as hard. I was just a kid, and my world fell apart."

Jill shook her head, and the long blond hair curled around her face. "I never guessed. You were so strong all through the sale and even the day of the auction. I kept waiting for you to cry, but you never did."

Ellie took a deep breath. "I never was one to cry."

"I know." Jill slowed the van to cross an autogate. Then she steered to the edge of the road as a pickup approached from the opposite direction. Half on, half

The Compromise

off the road, the vehicles passed one another. The older man driving the pickup waved to them, and Jill waved back.

Ellie smiled, then said a silent prayer: *God, please help me to stay strong. Help me to accept the past and to get on with my life. Thank you for the time I had on the ranch, and thank you for the person I am today.*

She was about to add a silent amen when Jill topped another hill and Ellie saw that they were almost there. To the north stretched a road that would lead them to Jill's family, and to the south lay the way to the home Ellie had once known.

"Thank you, Jill," Ellie whispered.

"For what?"

"For not taking the road past the old home place."

Jill reached for her hand, squeezed it gently, then crossed another autogate and came to a stop where the gravel road merged back onto the oil road. She turned right, and Ellie managed to blink back sudden tears. It was time to forget the past and look forward to Christmas.

As they pulled into the ranch yard and opened the van doors, Ellie grinned with the same excitement as everyone else. A tall, dark-haired man pulled Jill into his arms and hugged her tight.

"Good to have you home, sis."

"Good to be here, Mike," Jill said, and moved on to the rest of the family.

Mike came to Ellie next. "Long time, no see, cowgirl," he said, ruffling her short auburn hair with one hand before hugging her.

"I know." Ellie stepped back and looked up at him. "You're still as homely as ever, I see."

"You're still the flatterer."

Before Ellie could respond, a pretty woman with soft, shoulder-length brown hair joined Mike.

"Ellie, this is Jenny, the lady that took pity on a poor rancher and married me. That boy running in circles is Jenny's son, Peter."

"It's nice to meet you, Jenny." Ellie offered her hand.

"I've heard so much about you," Jenny said in a soft southern drawl.

"Don't judge me from that."

"Oh, I wouldn't dream of it. I've heard all about your famous fudge, and I'll wait to sample that before I make my decision."

Ellie grinned at the teasing and decided that Jenny was the perfect woman for Mike. The love in Mike's eyes as he looked at his wife and son affirmed her initial impression. She took one more glance around the ranch yard, then walked around to the back of the van where Jill and Brian were unloading the luggage. The air was near freezing, and she needed to don a coat or get busy to stay warm. She opted for the latter. Within

The Compromise

ten minutes, everything was unloaded, and the van was parked in the shed near the house.

The group chatted as they fixed lunch and ate. As they cleared the table, the sky grew overcast and gray. Only after the children were put down for naps and the adults gathered around the kitchen table with coffee did anyone notice the snow.

Ellie got up to add cold water to her coffee. She looked out the kitchen window at the meadow and lake. The hills across the valley were only dimly visible, and she forgot the coffee and the company as she stared at the wintery scene. Large white flakes were beginning to fall lazily from the sky, drifting down on the barest breath of wind.

"Ellie?" Jill said for the third time. Startled, Ellie turned around. The others were looking at her expectantly.

"It's snowing," she said.

At that, Jill raced to the window, and Ellie smiled at her enthusiasm.

"We're going to have a white Christmas after all!" Jill exclaimed in childlike delight.

Everyone laughed, and Ellie took her coffee back to the table. It didn't seem possible that tomorrow was Christmas Eve. Being back in the Sand Hills didn't seem possible either.

"I'm going to go see if the kids are awake. If they are, they'll want to see the snow," Ellie said. She set her coffee cup down and left the room as Mike turned to answer a question that Brian had asked.

"Peter's going to start kindergarten this January if we find a teacher."

Jill joined them again. "What do you mean, find a teacher?"

Jenny said, "Our teacher brought me her resignation yesterday. Her mother suffered a severe stroke, and there is no one else to care for her. She left for home today."

"We'll keep her in our prayers," Jill said softly.

"Keep the school in your prayers too," said Mike. "We're never going to find a teacher to finish out the term. It's hard enough to find someone in the fall, but in the dead of winter? I doubt there'll be anyone free to sign a contract and willing to come."

They fell silent for a moment, then Jill asked, "Is it still the same old one-room school we went to?"

"Last one-room school in the county," Mike told her proudly. "Remember how much fun we had?"

"I remember a certain pesky brother always tagging after me," Jill teased. "But we did have some good times."

"Peter was really looking forward to kindergarten," Jenny said. "But I can teach him enough at home to make up for not having school. The older children don't have that advantage. They will have to be driven to town all winter, and few of the parents can afford the time or gas. What really worries me though, is that if we

The Compromise

close the school, we may never get it opened again."

Jill bit her lower lip, gazing thoughtfully into her coffee cup. "We may have brought you a solution."

"What do you mean?" Jenny asked.

"Ellie. She just finished a teaching contract. If I understand correctly, she's free all spring. She's planning to substitute teach this spring and return to full-time teaching in the fall. She'd be perfect for the school. She went to it, after all, and she's taught several different grades, not at the same time, but I think she could handle it."

"And she grew up here," Mike said. "Living out in the middle of nowhere won't bother her like it does a lot of people."

"Should we speak to her?" Jenny asked. As the newly elected president of the school board, Jenny was in a position not only to speak, but also to make a decision.

"Maybe you should wait until after Christmas," Brian suggested. "I think coming back here has been stressful enough."

"We should," Jill agreed. "But we're short on time, and if she wants to think about it, she should have as much time as possible."

Mike nodded, and Jenny looked around the table. "I'll speak to her, then. If nothing else, perhaps she will know of another teacher suitable for the position."

"It's settled, then," Mike said with a grin. "Now, would anyone like some of the divinity that Peter and I made? It's guaranteed to cause a mouthful of cavities."

They all laughed. Mike went to fetch the plate of candy as Ellie walked back into the kitchen. She didn't notice each adult look up, evaluating her. They shared the latest joke, and she didn't know that they had measured her and found her worthy in every way. But then, the life she was about to begin would bring more surprises than that.

Chapter 2

The next morning, Jenny, Ellie and Jill prepared a hearty breakfast while Brian and Mike woke the children, straightened the house and started the laundry. After everyone had their fill of bacon, eggs and biscuits, the men took the three children and went to feed the cattle.

After loading the dishwasher, the women settled down at the table with cups of coffee and began planning Christmas Eve supper. They would open gifts that evening after reading the Christmas story and singing carols.

"Would you be willing to make your fudge, Ellie?" Jill asked, flipping through Jenny's recipe file.

"Certainly. It's been a while, but we can hope for the best."

"After watching Mike and Peter make candy, I'm ready for anything," Jenny said. "Other than more candy, all we really need to make is a batch of rolls and the chicken noodle soup. I have the cold cuts in the freezer, and I've hidden the crackers and cheese from

The Compromise

my guys. The fruit is in the cellar, and the candy is in the pantry."

"It sounds like a feast," Ellie said.

"Just a cold supper. Tomorrow we'll really earn our keep. I have the turkey thawing on the porch."

"What about lunch today?" Jill put the recipe file back on the island.

"I need to get some potatoes and green beans from the cellar, and we'll whip up a meatloaf," Jenny said.

"Oh, let me go to the cellar," Jill pleaded. "I'm just dying to get out and wade in the snow."

"Don't let me stop you," Jenny said with a laugh.

With a look of impish delight, Jill headed for the back porch. Ellie glanced at Jenny, and they both grinned as Jill closed the back door. Before she started mixing dough for the rolls, Jenny showed Ellie where to find a kettle and the ingredients for fudge.

"You have such a lovely home," Ellie said as she reached into the pantry for cocoa.

Jenny had decorated the entire house for Christmas, from the evergreen boughs wound through the banister to the towering tree in the living room.

"Thank you. I inherited the ranch from my grandfather about a year and a half ago. Mike and I were married six months ago."

"There's a story there," Ellie said with a smile.

"There is, and I'll tell you sometime, but right now, I need to ask you something."

"Sure, anything." Ellie measured cocoa and dumped it into the kettle.

"We lost our teacher two days ago, and ... well, Jill said you were free for the spring. Would you consider stepping in and teaching here, if not indefinitely, then at least until we can find someone else?"

"At Sweet Valley?" Ellie asked, referring to the one-room country school by the name it had earned years ago.

"Yeah. You would have nine students, ranging from Peter, who will just be starting kindergarten, to Christy, an eighth-grader. The school building is in good shape, and we have new textbooks and a lot of new equipment."

"Is there still a teacherage behind it?"

"No, it wasn't even fit for mice. We hauled it away last spring. Our teacher was driving about an hour each way from a little town north of here. She liked her little rental house too well to move, but we would provide housing nearby for you. We have two options, and if you take the job, then we'll work something out. At the most, you'd be nine miles away. The other option is a lot closer."

Jenny didn't go into details, but Ellie didn't care. "I would need to get a Nebraska teaching certificate."

"I'm sure you would be fine. What do you have now?"

"A standard Kansas elementary certificate." Ellie

The Compromise

thought of the immense task facing her and the board, if she should agree to the job. "I would have to move. Then I'd need at least a week to go through the books and get ready to teach. It would be pretty rough to start with, because I haven't done anything like this before. And the board would need to contact my references. I'd have to type a resume, and ..."

As her voice trailed off, Ellie's eyes lit up.

"Should I speak to the board after Christmas and arrange an interview?" Jenny asked softly.

Ellie turned from the cupboard to face Jenny, spoon still in hand. Her eyes sparkled, matching the brilliance of her smile, and Jenny suddenly realized that Ellie was a beautiful woman.

"Would you? I'd love to teach in that school."

"I would be glad to. But I must tell you, that as the president of the board, I'm already a little biased. After watching you with Peter, Beth and Emily last night, I know you're the woman I want in that classroom."

Ellie laughed with sheer joy and whirled back to the counter, attacking the chocolate mixture with renewed vigor. She had made the decision in haste, yet she had never felt surer about anything.

Jill brought in a bucket of potatoes from the cellar and glanced from one woman to the other. She whooped out loud. "You said yes, didn't you?"

"I said yes to applying for the job, I haven't been interviewed yet, and nothing's been offered ..."

"It doesn't matter!" Jill exclaimed, dropping the potatoes and hugging her friend tightly. "I know everything will work out for the best."

A contented Ellie joined the family that evening for supper, the reading of the Christmas story and finally the singing of carols. Even the children noticed a new brightness in her, and Jill had to remind herself that this was how Ellie used to be all the time. Later, the families gathered around the tree in the beautiful living room, and gifts were exchanged.

Ellie had purchased small gifts for each person, but she had expected little in return. She was surprised once again. Jill's family presented her with a set of antique teacups for her collection, while the gift from Mike and Jenny brought tears to her eyes. The saddle she unwrapped was none other than her own, the one sold at auction so many years ago.

"How, Mike?"

"I bought it at the auction that day with the intention of giving it back later, then you left without even saying goodbye. It's been out in the barn ever since, just waiting for the rightful owner to come claim it."

Ellie stroked the dark leather and breathed in the faint scent of horse, remembering. She would never forget this Christmas or the generosity of her friends. Her look of utter contentment reassured everyone that

The Compromise

bringing Ellie back to teach in the hills was the right thing to do.

As Jenny snuggled closer to Mike late that night, she realized that she had never been happier. She sighed gently and smiled to herself in the darkness.

"It's been quite a day, hasn't it?" Mike said softly.

"A wonderful day."

"Remember last Christmas?"

"How could I forget?" Jenny asked, eyes closed. "It was my second Christmas without David, and you were so good to Peter and me. Then you kissed me good night under the mistletoe at the back door."

"Just on the forehead. I loved you even then."

"Oh, Mike," Jenny whispered, "we've been so blessed."

"We have been. Now we'd better get to sleep. Morning comes early around here."

"I love you, Michael Snow."

"I love you too, honey. I really do."

Outside, the stars twinkled in an icy sky. The cattle slept peacefully in the hills and all was quiet.

Christmas came and went in a bustle of activity. The day after Christmas, Jenny began making her phone calls. Twenty minutes later, she stuck her head in the door of the bedroom where Ellie was playing with Emily and Beth.

"Ellie, the interview is tomorrow at three."

Ellie looked up. "That's fine. I'd like to type up a resume and application letter, too, if that would be OK."

Jenny grinned. "Sure. Use Mike's computer downstairs in the den." She turned her attention to the girls. "Peter wants to know if you two would like to go sledding with him. There's just enough snow on the hill to make it fun."

"Yeah, Aunt Jenny!" Emily cried, and Beth joined in. Jenny and Ellie took the girls downstairs and helped them find their coats. After the children were bundled up and sent outside, Ellie headed for the den.

The computer was on the desk in front of a wall of bookshelves. Ellie opened a word-processing program and began typing the information she knew by heart. Thirty minutes later, she pulled the final draft of the resume from the printer and looked it over, pleased with the result. The next letter was much harder to write. It took another hour to create a letter that she felt would do the job. Placing both papers in a folder, she went to the kitchen.

"Ellie, it's all ironed," Jill announced, holding the skirt aloft. Ellie took it from her, smiling gratefully.

The Compromise

"You didn't have to iron it, but I'm glad you did. You're a much better hand at the iron than I'll ever be."

"I have talented hands. You should see me sew up a patient. I make neat little stitches."

Ellie laughed, then turned her attention to dressing. She had less than an hour before the interview. The morning had passed quickly: Ellie had helped Mike feed the cattle, and they had returned home just in time for lunch. The afternoon had gone just as fast.

"Here, what do you think?" Ellie asked, buttoning the last button and turning for her friend's opinion.

"Beautiful, Ellie," Jill said, and she meant it. The cream-colored short sweater and long, flowing, dark-green skirt accentuated Ellie's trim figure. Brown suede boots finished the outfit, proving both pretty and practical. She looked stunning with her short auburn hair and dark-green eyes.

"This is just one of the things I brought to wear to church, but I think it will do." Ellie looked at herself critically in the full-length mirror, then grinned at Jill. "At the risk of sounding like a baby, I'm nervous."

"You'll calm down once you meet the board," Jill assured her. "Now get your coat and your papers. It's time to go."

It took about ten minutes to drive to the school. When Jenny turned the pickup off the main road onto the gravel road leading to it, Ellie gazed hungrily at the small building, then at the valley in which it sat. A ranch stood at the end of the valley. Haystacks stood tall in a distant stack yard and a curl of smoke rose into the air from the house.

"Who lives there now?" Ellie asked, pointing.

"A friend of Mike's – Zane Redding. Zane's uncle had the place before him, but I'm not sure who owned it before that."

"We did," Ellie said quietly.

Jenny glanced at her, but Ellie's face was only thoughtful. Pulling off the road to park at the school, Jenny saw that they were not the first to arrive.

"Laurie's here already. I guess that just leaves Anna."

They left the warmth of the pickup and walked toward the building. The sidewalk had been cleared of snow, as had the front step. Jenny held the door open for Ellie, then followed her in. Ellie stopped just inside the door, memories flooding back.

The cloakroom had changed little. The small entryway lined with coat hooks held a jacket already. Ellie slipped out of her own coat and hung it on the peg she had used all through school. Then she opened the door leading into the classroom.

This room had changed. The windows along the west wall were shaded with brightly colored miniblinds. The floor, which Ellie remembered as dusty hardwood, was covered with carpet. The desks were the same, as was

The Compromise

the old heater at the front of the room. But now a television and video cassette player sat to one side, as did a tape deck and a computer. Less than a minute passed as Ellie surveyed the room before she turned her attention back to Jenny and the other woman.

"Ellie, this is Laurie Richards, secretary of the board. Her oldest son, Jimmy, is in second grade, and her second son, Johnny, will be starting kindergarten with Peter. Laurie, this is Ellie MacCready."

"Hello," Ellie said, offering her hand. The woman looked enough like Jill to be her sister. Laurie's wide, welcoming grin quickly put Ellie at ease, and a moment later they welcomed the last member of the board, a quiet older woman whom Ellie remembered from her days on the ranch.

Gathered around the table under the windows, they finished exchanging pleasantries, and the interview began. Less than an hour later, Ellie stepped outside and walked around the playground as the three women inside made their decision. A few minutes later, Jenny stepped outside and asked Ellie to come in again.

"Well, Ellie," she said with a smile, "do you want to be our teacher?"

Ellie looked carefully at each woman, then smiled in return. "Where do I sign?"

Two days later, the van was packed and ready to go.

Brian, Jill, Emily, Beth and Ellie said their farewells. As final hugs were exchanged and everyone crawled into his seat, Jenny hugged Ellie one last time.

"We'll have a place for you to live when you get back. Either stop here or call ahead. And we'll have help to unload, too."

"Thank you so much, for everything."

"No, Ellie, thank you." Jenny squeezed her hand. "We'll see you soon."

The van door slid shut, and Brian started the engine. Looking back, they all waved one last time. Then they pulled out of the yard.

Unlike the time she left the hills eleven years ago, Ellie knew she would be coming back. Life had changed, and she was ready for it.

Chapter 3

The morning of January second dawned sunny and warm. The moving van, backed into the driveway, had the back open and was already half loaded. Ellie adjusted her grip on one corner of the piano and pushed for all she was worth, along with Jill, Brian and his friend Ty. A minute later, it slid into the truck, and Brian and Ty wrapped and tied it down.

"I can't believe you own a piano," Jill muttered fiercely. "And what about the washer and dryer? And the fridge? How many single women your age own their own appliances?"

"Quite a few, actually," Ellie said. "Besides, Jenny said that the place they have for me doesn't have a washer and dryer or a fridge. And as for the piano, I did minor in music."

"I know." Jill freed her hair and put it back into a ponytail, catching all the soft, blond locks straying about her ears. "I'm just thankful that Brian and I own our home and aren't planning on moving."

"Get a move on it, ladies!" Brian called as he and Ty

The Compromise

got out of the truck. "There's plenty left to carry that you can handle."

"I can carry anything that you can, mister!" Jill retorted, heading for the house.

Ellie followed as Brian said, "Prove it, woman."

In another hour, the rest of the furniture and the last of the boxes were loaded. Brian and Ty closed and locked the doors and volunteered to load Ellie's car onto the trailer and hook it behind the truck.

"I can't believe you're going to drive that rig clear to Nebraska," Jill said, looking at the truck.

"I'm not too worried about it. The weather's been fair, and the roads should be good."

Ellie walked through the door of the rental house one last time and looked around. She had spent two days packing. Jill and she had cleaned as the men loaded. Now all Ellie had to do was lock the door and leave.

"I'm going to miss you," Jill said suddenly.

Ellie looked at her friend. "I'll miss you, too. But I'm only a phone call away."

"I know." Jill wiped her eyes, then hugged Ellie tight. A horn honked, and they separated.

"I guess it's time to go." Jill took a ragged breath and shook her head. "You're strong, Ellie. You always were."

"Not as strong as I look," Ellie said, squeezing her hand. "Let's go."

She locked the door and slid the key under it.

Jo Maseberg

The moving van was parked on the street, and Ellie's little red sports car was on a trailer hitched behind it. After another round of hugs and a heartfelt thank you to all of them, Ellie climbed into the truck. Her overnight bag was on the floor of the passenger side, while her laptop sat safely in its case on the seat next to the cell phone.

Ellie buckled her seat belt, started the truck, waved and pulled away. Late that afternoon, she pulled off I-70 at Hays, Kansas. After buying gas and getting a bite to eat, she headed north, finally stopping for the night at a little motel in a small town in Nebraska.

Ellie was back on the road by eight the next morning and pulled into Ogallala at noon. After eating lunch, she spotted the truck rental place and made a quick decision. Pulling the truck into the parking lot, she unloaded the car and unhitched the trailer. She parked her car near the building and promised to return the truck later that afternoon. There was no sense in hauling the car down that road twice.

She left Ogallala, driving north over the dam that spanned Lake McConaughy. Reaching the last town before she would turn onto the oil road, Ellie picked up the cell phone and breathed a prayer of gratitude that it was still charged. She dialed Jenny and Mike's number and heard the phone ring twice before Jenny answered.

The Compromise

"Jenny, this is Ellie. I'm at the turnoff. I should be there in about an hour, or maybe a little over. Where do I go when I get there?"

"We've got it arranged. You'll be living in the little house at Zane Redding's ranch, just up the road from the school. Think you can find your way home all right?"

Ellie grinned. "You bet I can."

"We've got some people lined up to help you unload, too. We'll see you then."

"All right. See you soon. Bye."

Ellie punched the button on the phone and put the truck in gear. She turned onto the narrow road heading west.

"They take cattle trucks over this road," she said to herself. "I should be able to drive this thing."

An hour and fifteen minutes later, Ellie pulled into the ranch yard. She drove past the barn and corrals until she reached the first of two houses. The little one-story house with a front porch stood on its own lawn, surrounded by leafless trees and dead, scraggly flower beds. She had little time to stare. Four pickups were parked in the yard, and a group of people surged out of the house to meet her, Mike and Jenny in the lead. Ellie opened the door of the truck and reached for her coat, pulling it on as she jumped down.

"Where's your car?" Mike asked.

"Hello and how are you, too," Ellie said, teasing him.

"I left the car in Ogallala. I'll get it when I take the truck back."

"That works." Mike glanced at the truck, then at the house. "Do you mind if I back this up and we get started?"

"Go right ahead," Ellie said, stepping away, thankful for his offer.

"We thought that it would be easiest if they unloaded and you told them where to put things," Jenny said, steering Ellie toward the house. "Why don't we take a quick look around so you can get an idea of where you'll want things. Then the guys can get started."

"That sounds like a plan."

They went up the steps, across the porch and into the house. Memories came back as Ellie entered the living room, but she pushed them away to savor another time. A new, soft, rose-colored carpet had been put down. On the opposite wall, two doors stood open. Crossing the living room, Ellie poked her nose into the first door, a bedroom. The second door revealed the bathroom.

"The other bedroom opens into the dining room," Jenny said.

Ellie nodded, moving from the living room to the kitchen and dining room area. The kitchen cabinets had been painted white, and the walls were freshly painted as well. The floor was the same old tile that she remembered, and she smiled. The second bedroom door stood at the far end of the dining room area. She looked in. It

The Compromise

was a little smaller than the first bedroom, and it opened directly into the bathroom.

She paused a moment, getting her bearings. The two bedrooms were on the north, with the bathroom sandwiched between them, while the living room and the kitchen were on the south. On the east side of the kitchen was a covered back porch with hookups for a washer and dryer, and a coat rack. With the layout firmly fixed in her mind, Ellie rejoined Jenny at the front door. The men had the truck open, and Mike and another man were carrying her love seat up the steps.

"Where to?" Mike asked.

"There, under the window on the west," she directed. From then on, she had only to point, then turn to the next man coming through the door. The pace slowed when the men got to the piano. As they gathered around her, Ellie chose a spot.

"How about here, on the inside wall between the dining room and the living room, but not too close to the bathroom door."

The space was perfect. Fifteen minutes later, the piano sat against the wall, and the men finished unloading the truck. They hooked up the washer and dryer, plugged in the refrigerator, set up the bed and assembled her bookcases. When they finished, all that remained for Ellie to do was unpack the boxes, which were placed in the appropriate rooms.

"That ought to about do it," Mike said to Ellie as the

other men headed for their pickups.

"I don't know how to thank you guys, Mike," Ellie said, leaning against a porch rail.

"Do a good job with the kids, Ellie, and we'll call it even."

"Thanks again, Mike."

"What are you going to do now?"

"Take the truck back to town, get some groceries, come home and fall asleep."

"Well, it's only four-thirty. You should have plenty of time, as long as you don't mind driving after dark."

"Not a problem," Ellie assured him. "I'll just keep my eyes peeled for deer, cows and the occasional UFO."

As Mike and Jenny laughed, Ellie grabbed her purse and headed for the empty truck. She opened the door and was about to get in when she thought of something.

"Hey, Mike, where's my new landlord today?"

"Zane? I think he went to town for parts. You'll meet him later."

With a wave, Ellie pulled out of the yard and found herself on the road again. Turning up the radio, she sang along with the local country-music station, her heart lighter than it had been in years.

When she reached Ogallala, she returned the truck to the rental place and picked up her car. Ellie pulled into the street and quickly shifted gears, delighted to be back in her own vehicle. After supper at a local steak house, she went to the grocery store and stocked up. With

The Compromise

enough groceries for a month in the car, she started home again.

The dashboard clock read nine-thirty when Ellie pulled into the yard, drove up as close to the back door as she could get, unloaded the groceries and reparked the car along the back fence. She walked slowly back to the house, enjoying the nighttime sky. The lights in the big house across the yard were on, and Ellie wondered what Zane Redding was like. He's a friend of Mike's, so he must be nice, she thought.

"You're a lucky man, Zane Redding," she whispered. "You have everything that I want – the land, the cows, my home."

Now where did that come from? she wondered. Pushing aside all dangerous thoughts, she stepped into the warm house, closed the door firmly behind her and locked it. By the time Ellie finished putting the groceries away, she was more than ready for bed. She turned off the lights and moved to the bedroom.

The carpet was the same rose color as that in the living room, and the walls were white. Mike had set her bed up in the center of the north wall directly under a window. The other window was on the west wall. Ellie realized suddenly that neither window had curtains. After making up the bed, she searched for the box containing the various curtains she had made and bought over the years. Two pairs of white, ruffled curtains were on top, and they fit the room and windows perfectly.

She sorted out another set of curtains and hung them in the bathroom. Almost too tired to move, she got ready for bed and crawled beneath the covers.

As Ellie flipped off the bedside lamp, she snuggled down to say her prayers but fell immediately asleep, unable to push herself any further. A coyote howled in the darkness, but nothing disturbed her. She was home at last.

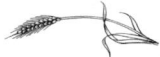

The morning light woke her, and Ellie stretched, looking around the small bedroom with satisfaction. The quilt on her bed in shades of pink, blue and white went well with the carpet and curtains. Her cherry wood double bed, dresser and nightstand just filled the room, especially with the way the closet jutted out on the east side of the door. She liked the room and remembered that she had some prints that would look nice on the walls.

Suddenly eager to explore the rest of the house, Ellie jumped out of bed and donned jeans and a sweatshirt. After stopping in the bathroom to fix her hair and brush her teeth, she stepped into the living room. Standing in the middle of the room, she turned slowly in a circle, taking it all in.

The love seat sat invitingly under the west window, which was curtainless.

One bookcase had been set between the love seat and

The Compromise

the south wall. The other one was on the south wall between the window and the corner. Beneath the south window, her glider and ottoman offered a comfortable seat and plenty of light for reading or crocheting. The piano filled the east wall, and the only furniture on the north wall was her entertainment center. Pleased with the arrangements, she moved to the kitchen.

The kitchen was as small as she had remembered. Still, she didn't need a lot of room. Cabinets lined the south wall and wrapped around to the east, stopping about three feet shy of the back door. The sink was under the window on the south wall, and there was plenty of counter space. Her refrigerator sat on the west wall and the stove was at the end of the counter near the back door. Her little drop-leaf table had been set up in the dining area on the north side of the kitchen. Ellie nodded and moved on to the smaller bedroom.

This room would be her office. Her desk and file cabinet had been set up. The closet would serve for storage and linens. After a quick look around, she drifted back into the kitchen to unpack enough dishes for breakfast.

"Three days," Ellie said. "I give myself three days to unpack and settle in. On day four, I go to school."

As she sat down with her bowl of cereal and a glass of juice, she bowed her head to give thanks. She had been blessed in so many ways.

"Thank you, Lord," she whispered. "Thank you so much."

Chapter 4

Ellie spent a week preparing for classes. At the end of the week, she knew that she could work for another month and still not feel prepared. School would start on Monday, however, and as she closed and locked the door to the school Saturday night, she promised herself that she would not enter the building on Sunday. She needed to be ready mentally and spiritually, as well as physically, and to do that, she needed to spend some time away from the schoolhouse.

Ellie walked a mile down the gravel road to her home. The air was getting chilly, and she was thankful for her warm parka and gloves. She breathed deeply and gazed thoughtfully at the hills and the cattle. It looked like Zane Redding had some fine animals. Her own family had run a mixed-breed operation, but Zane had all Angus cattle. Mike and he were the only two ranchers with Black Angus herds that she knew of in the immediate area. Others had Herefords or Charlois, and a few still raised mixed breeds.

Within a few minutes, Ellie realized that she was

The Compromise

already at the ranch yard. She walked past the empty corrals and headed for her little house. She had yet to see Mr. Redding up close. She often heard the tractor or saw the pickup, but she had not yet met the man. With her work to keep her busy, she just hadn't had time to track him down and introduce herself. She would no doubt meet him later. She had already formed a mental picture: He was older, balding, about fifty-five, and he wore flannel shirts and jeans, like an old bachelor cowboy.

"Oh well, Mr. Redding," she murmured to herself as she mounted the steps and opened the door, "you can wait; school can't."

Ellie put a pot of water on the stove for tea, then started a load of laundry. As the pot whistled, she dropped a tea bag into one of her dainty teacups and poured hot water over it. Just the scent warmed her. Finally, she settled into her chair with her Bible. She planned on watching a movie and going to bed early.

Due to the winter feeding schedules of the ranchers, the little country church didn't start services until two-thirty on Sunday afternoon. Ellie slipped into Mike and Jenny's pew a few minutes before the service and greeted them. She was surprised when Laurie Richards, one of the women who had hired her, stepped forward with a guitar and played the prelude. Afterward, the pastor stepped up to the pulpit.

"Thank you, Mrs. Richards. We appreciate all of you ladies taking turns and helping with the music, but we need to keep praying for a full-time pianist as well." He smiled kindly. "I would say organist, but we don't have an organ."

The congregation chuckled, then the pastor moved on to the other announcements and prayers. The sermon spoke directly to Ellie as the pastor spoke of God calling people to fill a need. As the service ended, Ellie rose and moved toward the door with the rest of the congregation. She shook hands with everyone. They all seemed to know who she was, but she had no idea who many of them were. Finally, she reached the pastor.

"And you must be the new teacher we've all been hearing about," the older man said with a smile.

"Yes, I'm Ellie MacCready."

"I'm Pastor Grey, and I hope to see you again next Sunday."

Ellie nodded and made her way to the door, at peace with herself and with the world.

The feeling of peace and satisfaction had fled by eight o'clock the following morning. She had been at the school since seven, preparing for classes. She didn't expect a lot to happen the first day, but she was anxious to meet the students and get to know them. In some

The Compromise

ways, she felt that she already knew them – their grades, artwork and reports told her a great deal. But these could not replace the need to see their faces and hear their voices.

Jenny brought Peter in at a minute past eight, holding him by the hand. She placed his lunch box on the shelf near the door and led him into the classroom. Ellie reminded herself that this wasn't only her first day; it was Peter's and Johnny's as well.

"Good morning, Peter." Ellie greeted him with a smile. "Are you excited?"

Peter nodded, suddenly shy, and Ellie took his hand. "Would you like to play with some blocks while we wait for school to start?"

She led him to the corner, then returned to Jenny.

"Any special instructions, Mom?" she asked as Jenny handed her Peter's backpack.

Ellie placed the bag beside Peter's seat as Jenny replied, "It's scary losing him to school so soon."

"I know. I promise to take good care of him."

Jenny nodded and tucked a lock of brown hair behind her ear. "I'll be back at three-fifteen. Goodbye, Peter."

"Bye, Mommy," Peter said, running to hug her. It was fortunate, Ellie thought, that Laurie brought Johnny and Jimmy in just then. Peter, spying two of his three best friends, immediately abandoned his mother and rushed to play with them. Laurie was lucky to get a quick hug before Johnny, too, had suddenly become unattached to his mother. The two mothers looked wistfully at their sons then left the building to go to their homes and help with the daily chores.

The rest of the students – four girls and two boys – arrived in a bunch. In no time, the clock read eight-fifteen, time to start school. Ellie rang the bell, and the students moved to stand beside their seats. She explained for the benefit of the younger boys that they would salute the flag.

"In fact," she said, turning to look at the rest of the students, "why don't we do things a little bit differently today. I'm going to say a line, then you repeat it back to me. Ready?"

Their faces were puzzled, but they seemed willing to try. Ellie grinned reassuringly, then turned to face the flag hanging from the wall above the blackboard.

"I pledge allegiance," she began, then waited for them to repeat it. Their voices were timid at first, then picked up strength and assurance. As they said the last line, they all looked fairly pleased with themselves, and Ellie knew she had made the right decision.

"Please take your seats," Ellie instructed. "I'm going to introduce myself and tell you a little bit about me, then I want each of you to do the same."

They nodded, and she began.

"My name is Miss MacCready, but you may call me Miss Mac. I moved here this winter from Kansas City, Kansas, where I taught school for several years.

The Compromise

Actually, I grew up on a ranch near here and went to school in this building."

They seemed surprised at that news, but she gave them no time to voice their opinions.

"Now, starting with the oldest, I would like you to tell me your name, grade level and at least one interesting thing about yourself. Christy?"

Christy Marcus, the one and only eighth-grader, sat up straight in her seat and strove to do her best. Ellie immediately pegged her as a good student and a hard worker.

"I'm Christy Marcus. I'm an eighth-grader, and I'm a barrel racer."

"Thank you, Christy. That was very good. Next?"

"I'm Drew Nichols, I'm a seventh-grader, and I ..." he paused, searching for something interesting. "I have two sisters."

Two girls in the desks in front of him grinned, obviously pleased that he had used them as his interesting fact. Drew seemed to be a devoted big brother, Ellie decided, and a kind, careful young man. Where Christy was petite and blond, Drew was tall and dark, already looking like a cowboy in his jeans and Western shirt.

"I'm Alex Klein," a boy with light-brown hair said from his desk next to Drew's in the back row. "I'm in sixth grade, and I have my own tractor. Oh, I have a sister, too."

"My name is Shayla Klein," a girl with pretty brown

braids said from her seat in front of Christy, "and I'm in fourth grade. I just learned how to bake bread by myself."

"I'm Kara Nichols, and I'm in fourth grade, too. I have a cat named Charlie." Kara looked a great deal like her older brother, although she seemed small next to Shayla.

"I'm Marcy Nichols. I'm in third grade, and I don't have a mother," Marcy announced. She seemed very self-assured.

"Marcy!" Kara hissed.

"It's the truth," Marcy responded, shrugging.

"That's enough, girls," Ellie told them, then turned to Jimmy. "Jimmy?"

"I'm Jimmy Richards, and I'm a second-grader. Dad's gonna give me my own calf this year for the fair."

Ellie grinned, then moved to stand before the last two desks in the front row. Peter and Johnny were both a little intimidated, but she saw that they were both excited.

"Johnny?" she prompted.

"I'm Johnny Richards, and I'm in kindergarten. I have a new bag, like Jimmy's, and my own lunch."

"Very good," Ellie said, then turned to Peter. His brown eyes were shining as he waited for his turn.

"I'm Peter Cook, but Mommy married Mike, so I'm gonna be Peter Snow soon. I'm in kindergarten, too, and I came from a long ways away, in Texas."

"Good." Ellie moved to stand in front of the teacher's

The Compromise

desk. "Now we're going to talk about some of the rules we should follow. I don't know how you did it before, but if anything I say sounds unreasonable, feel free to raise your hand, and I will call on you."

They were back to nodding, she saw, and she wondered if they were always so quiet and well-behaved.

"First off, you'll be using the same books and keeping the same schedule you had before, with one exception. We'll have music in the morning before we start the day." She saw the relief in their eyes at the reassurance that things would not change drastically.

"Next, if you have a question for me, raise your hand. If I do not see you, then quietly call me by name. If I'm working with another student, get up and come to me. I will help you as soon as I can.

"Third, if you need to use the bathroom, just get up and go. You do not need my permission. The same thing goes if you need a drink. All I ask is that you drink your water at the sink then put your paper cup in the trash. Please do not bring water back to your desk.

"Finally, if you need help, and I am clearly busy and will not be able to help for a while, go to someone older than you and ask. Alex, Drew and Christy, would each of you be willing to help a younger student?"

They nodded, except for Christy, who raised her hand.

"Yes, Christy?"

"Our last teacher didn't like us to help, so sometimes

people would wait with questions for an hour. I think your way sounds smarter."

"Thank you, Christy. That brings up something else. If you have to have my help, but I'm busy, put your book away and move on to your next subject. We'll come back to your question later, OK?"

At their affirmative nods and answers, she smiled again.

"Now, why doesn't everyone get out his or her reading books. Peter and Johnny, you can put your school supplies in your desks. Then hang your backpacks in the cloakroom, all right?"

As she moved from desk to desk assigning pages to be read and workbook pages to be completed, Ellie could only marvel at how smoothly the morning was going. The students were eager to learn and eager to please. No doubt the days to come would bring rough spots, but until then, she would enjoy the atmosphere.

At midmorning recess, all of the older students had finished their reading assignments, and most were halfway through math. The kindergartners had proven to her that they knew their alphabet, and she had listened to Jimmy Richards read aloud. As she pulled on her coat with the students, Ellie couldn't help but smile again to herself.

"Now, what do you usually do at recess?" Ellie asked as they jostled one another in the cloakroom, dressing in coats, hats and gloves.

The Compromise

"Whatever we want," Drew answered. "Usually the teacher would just stay inside and watch from the windows or something."

"Did you like that?" Ellie asked.

"It was OK, but sometimes it got boring." Drew knelt to fasten Peter's coat. Ellie watched in silent amazement as Christy went around to each younger student and checked to make sure that hats and gloves were on properly.

"All right, how about this?" Ellie proposed. "I will suggest an activity or game for morning and afternoon recess, but you may do as you like over the lunch hour."

"Will you play too?" Kara asked.

"Sometimes," Ellie promised. "I think I'll play today."

"Play what?"

"How about ..." Ellie paused, recalling a game she had played as a student. "How about freeze tag, and ... Alex, you're it."

As she headed out the door with her charges, Ellie couldn't help but feel grateful that she had dressed in corduroy pants and hiking boots for the first day of school. Running through the short prairie grass and sandburs would have ruined the dresses she had worn in Kansas City. Things had changed in more ways than one, she mused, but she loved it already. Somehow, she had known she would.

Chapter 5

The end of January came quickly, and Ellie's life settled into a pattern of sorts. She rose early, got to school by seven-thirty and left school at four or four-thirty. In the evenings, she fixed supper, graded papers and played the piano. Often she would bundle up and take a short walk.

On the last Friday night of January, the phone rang. The sound startled her, and it took Ellie a moment to realize what it was before she answered it.

"Hello?"

"Hi, Ellie, it's Mom. I haven't heard from you in forever."

Hearing the worry in her mother's voice, Ellie did her best to sound reassuring. "I've been really busy with school, that's all." She stretched the phone cord from the far side of the living room to her favorite chair and settled in.

"How is it going?"

"Really well. The kids are so sweet. Yesterday, Christy listened to Peter read aloud, then read both the kin-

The Compromise

dergarten boys a story. I don't have a single troublemaker in the lot – just a bunch of really nice kids."

"If you'd marry and settle down, you could have some really nice kids of your own."

Ellie laughed. "Mom, I'm twenty-eight. If I haven't found him by now, I'm not going to. Or if I do, it will be at the right time. God is looking out for me."

"I wish He'd look a little faster," her mother grumbled.

"Yes, Mom. So, how's Dad?"

"Oh, you know him. He's at work in the shop again."

Ellie twisted the phone cord around the arm of the chair and leaned back, closing her eyes. It felt good to hear her mother's voice. School was going well, but she was exhausted. Eventually, things would settle down. Until then, however, she took her leisure moments when and where she could get them.

When she finished talking with her mother, Ellie took a long, hot bath and went to bed, hoping to get about twelve hours of sleep. But that was not to be.

At five o'clock Saturday morning, headlights flashed through the living room windows and shone into Ellie's open bedroom doorway. The lights themselves would not have bothered her if it hadn't been for the sound of engines gearing down and the din of cattle bawling. In horror, she sat upright in bed. Grabbing a warm robe, she ran for the back porch, the only room with windows facing the barn and corrals. At first, she stared in disbelief, then comprehension dawned as Zane Redding's entire calf herd milled around in the corral.

"Sale day," she whispered to herself. "He's going to sell his calves today."

With that mystery cleared up, Ellie headed back to bed, a little sorry that she would not be going. She had loved sale day and the noisy, crowded sale barn. "You haven't got any cows, girl," she reminded herself. "And you need your sleep."

Still, as she snuggled underneath the warm quilts, she couldn't help but feel a little left out. "Have a good day, Mr. Redding," she whispered softly as her eyes closed again.

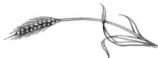

"It looks like we got it all taken care of," Mike said to Zane as the last truck pulled away from the loading chute two hours later.

"Thanks, Mike." Zane shook his friend's hand. "I couldn't have done it without you."

"Hey, you helped me last fall."

"Sure, but I didn't want to mention it."

Both men laughed.

Mike gestured after the trucks. "Looks like you'd better get dressed and follow those trucks to town. I'll take care of your feeding."

The Compromise

"Are you sure?"

"Yep. I know where everything is. Besides, I need to go say hi to your neighbor. She'd shoot me if she heard I didn't stop, but you've probably learned all about that temper of hers by now, huh?" Mike teased.

Zane shook his head. "To be honest, I haven't even met the woman."

"You haven't even seen her?" Mike asked, incredulous.

"Nope. What's to see? Another sweet, middle-aged schoolmarm from the city without a clue about the real world? No, thank you. I've got a lot more serious things to worry about – like keeping this ranch afloat."

"It's your decision," Mike said, shaking his head. "I'll see you later."

Zane nodded and walked briskly past the schoolteacher's house toward his own. He hadn't been entirely truthful with Mike. He had seen the woman, from a distance. She liked to walk in the evening, all bundled up in a shapeless coat and bulky hat. He'd never spoken with her, but he knew all he wanted to know. He'd heard her classical music in the evening, and he'd seen her sports car. An overeducated spinster was not the kind of person he needed for a friend. Besides, as he had told Mike, he had bigger things to worry about.

Dressing in his good jeans, dress boots and a new Western shirt, he grabbed a bite of breakfast then headed to town in his old pickup, waving at Mike as he left the yard. Zane caught up with the cattle trucks about ten miles down the road and followed them to town.

Mike watched Zane leave, then headed out to feed the cattle. It was after nine when he got back. He decided that was late enough and strode up the path to Ellie's front door. He knocked briskly and was surprised when she opened the door almost immediately. Dressed in jeans and a college sweatshirt, she had a dust rag in one hand.

"Hey, Mike. What brings you by?"

"I just helped Zane sort and load the calves for the sale. Today's his big day."

"Yeah, I noticed," Ellie said wryly, stepping aside and gesturing for him to enter. "Come in and stop letting the heat out."

"I can't. I'm in the middle of feeding for Zane, then I'm going home to do my own. I just wanted to say hi and ask if you'd like to spend the afternoon – or what there will be left of it after feeding's over – with Jenny. Peter's visiting at Laurie's, and Jenny said she'd like to see you. She said to tell you that your saddle's waiting for you in the barn where you left it. She wanted to know if you would like to go for a ride."

"I'd love to. Why don't I help you feed? An extra set of hands might make things go a little faster."

"It might at that," Mike admitted. "But you don't have to."

"I can still open a gate," Ellie said as she turned to put

The Compromise

away the dust rag and get her heavy coat. "And I'm pretty good with a pitchfork."

An hour and a half later, they finished feeding Zane's cattle. Ellie had kept her part of the bargain, opening gates and driving as Mike fed out the hay. Her cheeks were red from the cold air, but her blue eyes sparkled happily. Mike couldn't help but wonder what Zane's reaction would be if he saw Ellie in action. Somehow he doubted if Zane would have sounded quite so scornful or careless when speaking of the schoolteacher.

"Just let me grab my boots," Ellie yelled as Mike headed for his pickup. "I'll be right back."

True to her word, she hopped into the cab of the pickup and fastened her seat belt moments later. "I'm ready. Do you suppose Jenny will have lunch on?"

"Grow up, Ellie," Mike said as he put the pickup in gear. "Stop thinking with your stomach."

His stomach chose that moment to growl loudly.

Ellie looked at Mike, her eyes brimming with laughter. "There really has to be a comment," she said mirthfully, "but I think we'll just let your stomach speak for itself."

Jenny had lunch ready when they arrived. The three ate hungrily, then set out to feed. With more than four hundred head of cattle, Mike and Jenny's feeding took quite a bit longer than Zane's, but they finished before three. As Mike headed toward the shop to tinker with the pickup, Jenny and Ellie returned to the house. Jenny brewed a pot of tea, and they sat comfortably at the table, savoring the warm drink.

"I had hoped that we could go for a ride since the weather is so nice," Jenny said, feet propped on a chair.

"I'm up to it," Ellie told her.

"I'm not sure I am. I've been pretty tired lately." Jenny placed her mug on the table and rubbed her eyes. "In fact, I could really use a nap."

"Then why don't we just find comfy chairs and talk?" Ellie asked.

"If that's a motion, I second it."

They moved to the living room, Jenny claiming the couch. Ellie curled up in a big armchair and watched as Jenny got comfortable, covering up with an afghan and propping pillows behind her head.

"Ah, this is much better," Jenny said, her eyes drifting shut.

"Are you going to sleep or talk?" Ellie asked with a grin.

"I can do both."

"Tell me a story then."

"Anything?"

Ellie shifted position, tucking her feet beneath her. "Tell me how you met Mike."

"Oh ..." Jenny's voice trailed off, and for a moment, Ellie feared that she was asleep. Then she spoke. "Well,

The Compromise

here goes. I'd better start at the beginning, or it won't make any sense.

"The ranch was my grandfather's. My father never had an interest in running it, and that caused hard feelings between the two, but I was allowed to visit during the summer. When I was about sixteen, though, I had words with my grandfather. He refused to allow anyone to help him with the ranch. He was getting older and weaker every year, and he wouldn't trust anyone. My parents wanted him to sell and move to town. But he refused.

"I loved him and only wanted the best for him. Even with all my summers on the ranch, I never knew what it was to love the land until now, and I could not understand why he would not just sell it like ... like some old used car that had outlived its usefulness. He tried to tell me, but I wouldn't listen. I left angry, and I never returned. I went to college, met David, married and had Peter.

"Then David died. Worse yet, it was the night before Thanksgiving. He had driven to the airport to pick up Mom and Dad. On his way back, he ... he was hit by a drunk driver. All three died instantly." Jenny's voice broke, and Ellie felt like crying with her.

"Oh, Jenny, I'm so sorry."

"It was awful, but the worst part came later. I had to get a job, and it didn't last. I sold everything. I was down to my last dime and ready to call Grandfather for help when the lawyer called and said my grandfather was dead. He'd left the ranch to me. Somehow Peter and I came north. I met Mike at the funeral. He helped me get home, and the next day he came to check the windmills.

"He was here every time I needed him. He helped me sell my calves, and we made a bargain. I promised to cook him dinner if he would help me feed.

"Ellie, it was the most awful winter we've had in years. We pulled together, and somehow we made it through. In the spring, we discovered that we had fallen in love. We married right out there in front of the house, and we've been a family ever since."

"That's a wonderful story, Jenny."

"I've been so blessed. God has given me two wonderful men to love. What about you, Ellie? Have you found the right one yet?"

"No," Ellie said seriously. "I've dated a few nice guys, but I've never found the right one. Whoever he is, though, he's someone special. My mom doesn't think I'll ever meet him, but I know he's there. I just have to be patient."

Jenny nodded, eyes still closed. After a few moments of silence, she said, "And on a different note, what do you think of Zane?"

"Mr. Redding?"

"Yup."

"Actually, we haven't met yet."

The Compromise

"You're kidding!" Jenny sat upright on the couch and turned to look at Ellie.

"Nope. I've seen him from a distance – he drives by once in a while – but I haven't had a chance to speak to him or see him up close."

"Aren't you curious?"

"Well," Ellie said candidly, "I figure he's probably fifty something, wears flannel shirts and tells stories. Am I close?"

Jenny laughed outright. "That bad, huh? I'd better tell you, before you mistake someone else for him and get in a lot of trouble," Jenny said, still laughing.

"Zane Redding is twenty-nine years old. He stands about six feet one inch in his socks, and looks like a lean, old-time cowboy. He's got sandy hair and gray eyes, and he's fairly closemouthed unless you know him well. His dad's a vet near Valentine, and his mom's a school nurse. He grew up working for his uncle in the summer on his uncle's ranch.

"His uncle sold his first ranch and bought yours from your parents. Zane was almost done with college when his uncle died in a nasty accident, and Zane inherited the ranch. He doesn't talk much about it, but I know he loved his uncle very much.

"Anyway, Zane finished college and came here. After he paid the inheritance taxes, he didn't have much left for operating money, but he made it through some pretty lean years. Then he started changing his herd from

Jo Maseberg

Hereford to Angus, which wasn't cheap. I think he has a fairly large debt because of it, but if you ask him, he'll say it's worth every penny."

Jenny paused and looked closely at Ellie before continuing, gauging the effect of her words.

"The reason you haven't met him probably isn't because he's shy, but because he's working fifteen-hour days trying to keep body and soul together. When he's not babying those cows, he's in the shop, trying to keep equipment that's older than he is running, without spending a fortune. He's a good man, Ellie, and he loves that land as much as or more than you do."

"I didn't know," Ellie whispered.

Everything began to fall into place. Ellie thought of the straight barbed-wire fences she'd seen on her walks, of the neatly patched roofs and walkways on the place. He was trying hard to make it work.

Late that night, as Mike crawled into bed, he remembered something he had forgotten to tell his wife.

"I talked to Zane this morning, and he said he hadn't met Ellie yet."

"That's what she said," Jenny murmured.

Mike pulled the covers up and settled in. "That's not the good part. He thinks Ellie's a spinster schoolteacher with a city background wanting to play house in the country for a few months."

The Compromise

"He said that?"

"Not exactly, but that's what I picked up."

"Did you set him straight?"

"Nope."

"I did tell her the truth," Jenny said. "She thought he was fifty, overweight and long-winded."

"Seems to me they're perfect for each other."

"Now, Mike, we can't play matchmaker; it just isn't fair."

"Sure it is. However, I will turn it over to God. With God on our side, how can we lose?"

Jenny laughed despite herself and cuddled close. Indeed, turning it over to God was the best decision. After all, that had worked for them, hadn't it?

Chapter 6

The month of February came and went. Ellie spent long hours at school, but she also made time for herself. She visited Mike and Jenny often, and as other families in the community invited her to dinner, she got to know them as well. She organized a party for Valentine's Day, and the students sang songs while she played the piano.

Scattered snow flurries broke up the cold, sunny days. On snowy days, Ellie watched it fall from the windows of the school, and sometimes she saw a tractor pulling a loaded hay sled at the far end of the valley. On those days, she wished to be home, baking a batch of bread and tending children – her own children.

The first week of March, the sun shone fiercely, and temperatures rose to nearly fifty during the day. Ellie made sure that her class spent as much time outside as possible. Calving season would be coming soon, and when it did, she had no doubt that the weather would deteriorate.

Ellie wasn't the only one looking forward to calving. Zane had his hands full as he began to clean and ready

The Compromise

the calving barn. Trouble struck early one Saturday morning when the pickup broke down yet again. As he walked the mile back to the house, Zane's good mood went quickly downhill. By the time he reached the shop, he wasn't fit company for anyone – even himself.

With a sinking feeling, he saw that he was not the only early morning walker. The schoolteacher was out as well, and she was headed straight for him. Of all times to meet her, it had to be today.

Glancing both ways, he wondered if he could change course and somehow avoid her, but she was too close. With a sigh, he decided to make the best of it. The school was paying him a fairly substantial amount to house the woman, and it wouldn't do to get her, or the board, angry. He stopped looking for escape routes and turned his attention to her.

"Good morning!" she called cheerfully as she neared him. "Did you have a nice walk?"

He stared at her, his mouth dropping open for a full second before he snapped it shut again. Why hadn't he been warned? Why hadn't someone said something? This woman was the most unschoolteacherlike person he had ever seen in his life. From the top of her endearing, short, wispy auburn curls to the bottoms of her neat little hiking boots, she was beautiful.

"A what?" he finally managed.

"A walk," she repeated. "I had the binoculars out, bird-watching, and I saw you hiking in. I thought I'd come and see if you needed any help."

"Oh, yeah. The pickup broke down again. I just need to get the tractor and go pull it back."

She nodded and stuck out her hand. "By the way, I'm Ellie MacCready."

"Zane Redding," he responded, shaking her hand. He felt steel in her grip, belying the soft whiteness of her hands. "Well, I'd better go get the tractor."

"Nice to meet you."

He had made it five feet when she came running up beside him. "Listen, if you're going to pull the pickup back, don't you need somebody to steer it and brake? Because, if you do, I've got some time ..."

She sounded so earnest. Looking down into her green eyes, he realized that she was really sincere.

Surprising himself, he said, "I'd appreciate the help."

As they continued on to where the big feeding tractor was parked, Zane discovered that another of his assumptions about her was wrong. Ellie didn't pester him with needless questions. Instead, she walked along by his side with an easy stride, in comfortable silence. Reaching the tractor, he swung up and sat on the only seat. Ellie climbed in behind him and perched on the three-inch-wide shelf beneath the side window. The tractor roared to life, and Zane put it in gear.

As they neared the barbed-wire gate that led to the cow pasture, Ellie touched his shoulder gently. "I'll get the gate."

The Compromise

He didn't have time to question her experience or expertise. As soon as he stopped the tractor, she leaped lightly to the ground and trotted to the gate as if she knew what she was doing. Watching her, Zane could see that she did know. She grasped the metal lever holding the gate closed, unclipped the bar from the top wire of the gate, let it swing free and hauled the gate open.

As Zane drove through and halted on the other side, he looked back and yelled, "Leave it open. We'll get it on the way back."

She nodded, dropped the gate on the ground and climbed back into the tractor.

"That was pretty good," Zane said.

"Thanks. Mike's been letting me practice," Ellie said with a laugh.

As they rounded the next hill, Zane saw that the cows had crowded around the pickup, expecting their feed.

"I didn't get the cake fed before I broke down," he said.

"Hadn't we better feed them before we try to get the pickup back?" Ellie asked. "Otherwise, they're liable to follow us all the way back to the shop."

"Yeah. The question is, how? I'd just walk along and dump the cake, but these old girls aren't that tame. I'd probably get run over." Zane looked the situation over for a minute, the tractor idling. "Would you be comfortable steering the tractor if we hooked the pickup up behind it and I fed out of the back of the pickup?"

"I can do that."

"Good." They grinned at each other, and Zane's bad mood melted away.

Ellie stood up, reaching for the door. "I'll go shoo the cows away while you back the tractor up to the pickup."

Before he could warn her about the skittishness of the cows, she had leaped down once again and was moving toward the pickup and the hundred-plus cows that were gathered around it.

"Come on, girls, time to move," he heard her call. She made no sudden movements. Instead, she walked purposefully toward the front of the pickup. When Zane saw that she had things under control, he turned to his own task, pulling the tractor up to a position ahead of the pickup before putting it in reverse.

In five minutes, they had the pickup chained to the tractor. Zane gave Ellie quick instructions on how to put the tractor in gear and what to watch for while pulling the pickup. As he did so, he said a silent thank-you that the pickup had broken down facing a long, mostly flat area that would give them few problems as they fed.

After Ellie assured him for the fifth time that she could handle it, Zane jumped down from the tractor and headed for the pickup. He slid into the seat and took the pickup out of gear before closing the door and climbing into the bed of the truck. Once he was stand-

The Compromise

ing in the back, beside feed sacks full of cottonseed cake, he gave her a thumbs up, and she put the tractor into gear. He heard the throttle increase, and the tractor began to move slowly, taking up the slack in the chain. When the chain became taut and the tractor felt the weight of the pickup, Ellie increased the throttle. Everything worked so smoothly that the pickup was moving before Zane was ready for it.

The mooing and bellowing of the hungry cattle brought him back to Earth. He picked up a feed sack, stepped to the side of the pickup and began to scatter the cake. The long, rounded cubes of dark-brown, pressed cottonseed hit the ground, bounced and were devoured by the cows. Emptying one sack, Zane reached for another. By the time he reached the last sack, the cows were spread out along a quarter of a mile, heads to the ground, snuffling for pieces they had missed. He grinned, feeling pride in the herd he had built. Turning, he waved at Ellie to stop, and he jumped out of the back of the pickup. He jogged to the driver's door, opened it, slid into the seat and stepped on the brake as the tractor came to a halt.

They met between the vehicles and paused for a moment.

"You have some nice-looking cows," Ellie said.

"Thanks."

As Zane took his seat on the tractor and prepared to pull the pickup back to the house, he couldn't help but wonder why he hadn't made time to meet the new schoolteacher sooner.

"Me and my stupid assumptions," he said aloud in the noisy cab of the tractor. Still, first impressions weren't always right. She was, after all, a city girl. She had come from the city and would no doubt be returning to the city when school was out in the spring.

"You've got enough trouble already, without getting involved with her," he told himself sternly. "Keep your mind on the ranch and off the lady."

When Zane pulled up to the shop, he unhooked the tractor and waited as Ellie put the pickup in gear and got out.

"I've got to finish feeding now. It was nice to meet you, Ellie. Thanks for your help."

"I was glad to do it, Mr. Redding. If you ever need anything, feel free to knock on my door."

"OK, Ellie, and call me Zane."

He forgot all of his good intentions as she grinned at him in pleasure, then turned and walked away.

"She won't stay," he told himself as he got into the tractor and started toward the stack yard, where the hay sled waited. Still, the thought of her could not keep him from whistling cheerfully for the rest of the morning.

The Compromise

Ellie returned to her house and completed her housework before eating a light lunch. As she finished washing dishes, the telephone rang. She dried her hands and picked it up.

"Hello?"

"Ellie, it's Jenny. Would you care to go for that ride this afternoon?"

Ellie grinned. "I'd love to."

"Good. See you in about an hour?"

"An hour," Ellie agreed. "Goodbye."

Ellie hung up the phone and set the stove timer for thirty minutes. She had a stack of workbooks to grade over the weekend, and the sooner she got started on them the better.

When the timer rang, she looked up. She had graded about half of what she had to, a feat she considered more than fair. She headed toward the back porch to get her boots, coat, gloves and hat. She stood for a moment, gazing at the boots, remembering. The heels were worn down, the brown leather scuffed and worn in places. They fit her to perfection, though, and she wouldn't trade that feeling for any amount of polish and shine.

As she walked across the yard to her car, she saw that the tractor was back and the shop doors were open. Zane was no doubt working on the pickup.

Jenny's description of Zane had hardly done him justice, Ellie decided as she started the car and drove out of the yard.

He looks young to be carrying the burden of the ranch, and yet his gray eyes seem so old, Ellie thought. At least Jenny told me what to expect – poor Zane had not had a clue. I don't know what assumptions he'd made about me, but apparently I didn't match any of them. The look on his face when we met was priceless.

An hour later, Jenny and Ellie stood in front of the barn, untying their newly saddled horses. Jenny led her horse toward the gate, and Ellie followed. Once on the road, they mounted up. As Ellie put her foot in the stirrup and gathered a handful of mane, she couldn't help but wonder how she had ever left the ranch. Everything was falling into place so easily now that she was back.

In one fluid movement, she stepped up and swung her leg over the saddle. Gathering the reins, she waited until Jenny was seated, then both women nudged their horses into a walk, headed for the meadow.

"How do you like Thorne?" Jenny asked. The saddles creaked comfortingly, and the wind was little more than a gentle breeze. White, puffy clouds skidded across a blue sky, and the brown hills around them were beautiful.

"He's a complete gentleman," Ellie said, patting the dapple-gray gelding's neck. "Red's not too bad, either."

"Red and I have an understanding. He minds his manners, and I mind mine," Jenny said with a laugh.

The Compromise

"I like that idea."

"How about a faster pace for a bit?" Jenny suggested.

"All right, but I must warn you that I haven't ridden in so many years it's not even funny. I'm going to be sore tomorrow."

"You don't need to warn me. You'll be the one in pain."

With more laughter, they moved their horses into a trot, then a smoother lope, slowing only when they reached the pasture gate on the east side of the meadow. Ellie was glad when they halted, and gladder still that the gate was open so they didn't have to dismount.

"I'm feeling those muscles already, Jenny," Ellie said as they rode into the pasture and started up the first hill.

"We'll take it slow. Just enjoy the day."

"I intend to."

They rode in silence for several minutes, then Jenny asked, "Did you ever meet Zane?"

"Yes, just this morning, in fact. I helped him tow the pickup back to the shop."

"First impressions?"

"Hmm. Well, very handsome, but don't get any matchmaking ideas," Ellie said quickly. "I do believe, however, that he was expecting someone else. The poor man's jaw dropped open, and he stood there staring down at me like he'd never seen a woman before."

"Just wait until Mike hears this," Jenny said, laughing.

Jo Maseberg

Peter and Mike were playing a board game when the phone rang. Mike answered it, gesturing for Peter to turn the spinner.

"Hey," he said.

"Mike?"

"Hi, Zane." Mike stretched the phone cord across the kitchen and took his turn, moving his piece four spaces.

"I met the new schoolmarm this morning."

"Yeah?"

"Why didn't you warn me?" Zane asked seriously.

"Warn you?"

"Mike, my jaw dropped, and I stood there gulping like a fish, staring at the poor woman."

"Probably that red hair, huh?" Mike asked sympathetically, watching Peter play.

"Oh, the red hair, the green eyes, the nice figure, or maybe the fact that she can open a gate like greased lightning."

Mike dropped all pretense as he gave his friend the best advice he could. "Zane, she's everything you've met and more. Don't sell her short."

"I'm not going to do anything with her, Mike. I can't afford to get involved. What's here for a woman like her? She'll go back to the city one of these days, and I don't intend to get hurt when she leaves."

A moment later, they said their farewells and hung

The Compromise

up. Mike stared at the phone for a second, wondering how Zane would feel if he knew the truth about Ellie. He really should have told him, or at least hinted at it. Still, it would be better if Ellie told him herself. A little more conversation between the two might not be a bad thing.

"Your turn," Peter said.

"All right. Sorry about that, Peter."

"That's OK. We've got lots of time."

Indeed. Time was a luxury he could afford.

Chapter 7

By the end of March, calving was in full swing. Ellie's students proudly told her how they had witnessed the miracle of birth in the pasture or the calving barn, and she shared their excitement. Despite the joy of the season, she knew that calving also brought with it long days and longer nights. And deep down, she worried about Zane.

At the beginning of calving, Zane had moved his cows into the pasture just behind the house, where they would be close to the barn. He checked them every few hours day and night, just in case a cow was having trouble giving birth. If she was having trouble, he'd herd her into the calving barn and help with the delivery. If the situation was out of his control, he would call the vet.

Only once had Ellie seen the pickup with the vet's paraphernalia in the yard. Still, she worried; she knew the hectic schedule had to be taking its toll on Zane. She remembered when she was a girl, the whole family had pitched in during calving season, and although the bur-

The Compromise

den had been shared, it had been tiring for them all.

As Ellie crawled into bed one night, she said her usual prayers and added a special one for Zane and the ranch before drifting off into a dreamless sleep.

Zane found the heifer on his midnight check. The weather was gradually deteriorating, and the icy wind was beginning to howl from the north. It cut through his thick coveralls and coat, numbing his cheeks and bringing tears to his eyes. The majority of the herd was huddled in the shelter a hill provided. Most of the cows were lying contentedly, chewing their cud. As he drove slowly by, Zane noticed a heifer off to one side, snuffling the ground, tail raised. She was obviously in labor, but a closer look with the flashlight revealed something more.

"Come on, girl," he said as he turned the pickup off and got out. "It's time to get you to the barn."

Thankfully, she was within a quarter mile of it. Zane moved cautiously, wary. If she showed signs of chasing him, he could drive back to the barn and get the saddle horse. Either way he was going to get her to the barn.

As he neared her, she rolled her eyes and started walking awkwardly away from him in the direction of the corrals and the barn. Twenty minutes later, Zane herded her into a corner of the barn and closed a panel after her.

With her head firmly in the head gate, he moved to her back end and checked her progress. Things were worse than he feared. The tiny emerging hooves were upside down.

"You'll be all right, girl," Zane told the heifer reassuringly as she began to struggle. "I'm gonna help you."

He stripped off his coat, rolled up his sleeves and donned a long plastic glove. The calving barn was warmer than it was outside and protected from the wind, but it was still chilly. After a few minutes of attempting to turn the calf, Zane knew he was in trouble. His arm was too big for the heifer. If he didn't do something soon, he would lose the calf.

I can't afford to lose a calf, he thought as he stripped off the glove and reached for his coat.

Once dressed, he jogged to the house to call the vet. He could ill afford the cost of the vet's visit, but the calf and the heifer were worth far more.

As he entered the house, he flipped on the lights and reached for the phone. It took him a second to notice the utter silence of the line. No dial tone. Of all times for the phone lines to go out.

What next? He paused, thinking quickly. Ellie. Maybe her phone worked, although he doubted it. Still, even if it didn't, maybe she would go for the vet.

Zane jogged up her front walk to her door. He took a deep breath and pounded on the door.

The Compromise

A voice yelling her name jerked Ellie from a sound sleep. She sat upright, reaching for the bedside lamp and her robe. Opening the front door, she saw Zane looking haggard and cold.

"What's wrong?" she asked quickly.

"One of my heifers is havin' trouble calving. My phone is out. Does yours work?"

"Come in," Ellie said, "and shut the door behind you. I'll check the phone."

She ran for the phone and picked it up. There was only silence.

"It's out!" she yelled, then saw that Zane stood at the kitchen door, his broad shoulders filling the narrow doorway.

"Would you go get the vet for me? I can't leave the heifer."

"I've got a better idea," Ellie said, turning. On the cupboard by the microwave sat a small black stand with her cell phone, a green light indicating that it was charged and ready to go. "This should do the trick." She turned it on and handed it to him. "Just dial normally then press talk."

"I don't know how to thank you."

Zane dialed the vet's number from memory, moving out of the doorway so Ellie could pass him.

Back in her bedroom, Ellie closed the door and reached for jeans, a T-shirt and a sweatshirt. In less than a minute, she was warmly dressed.

Opening the door, she heard Zane say, "Hold on a sec, I'll go look and call you back."

Ellie grabbed her coat from the rack and followed Zane from the house. He had the cell phone in one hand and a flashlight in the other.

"The vet wants me to tell him how it looks right now," Zane explained as Ellie walked swiftly beside him.

Inside the barn, Ellie saw why Zane was worried. As he dialed the vet again and began describing the situation, she stroked the heifer soothingly.

"It's gonna be all right, girl," Ellie crooned. "We'll help your baby."

"Doc, I can't get my arm inside her!" Zane said in frustration.

Ellie reached out to touch his arm. Zane turned, and she said softly, "I can get my arm in."

"Hold on a minute, Doc," Zane said, then covered the mouthpiece with his hand. "You don't know what to do, even if you can get your arm inside."

"Yes I do," she said. "I've done it before. Give me a sleeve, and I'll do what I can. If we wait for the vet, it will be another hour, and he'll probably end up doing a C-section. If we can do this without cutting her open, it would be best."

Zane nodded, then spoke into the phone again. "OK,

The Compromise

Doc, I've got a lady here who says she can do it. I'll give you a call back if this doesn't work."

Zane ended the call and reached for the box of plastic gloves. Ellie stripped off her coat and hung it over a nearby panel. She took another look at the heifer then stripped off her sweatshirt. She took the glove from Zane and pulled it on. Without further ado, she eased her hand inside the cow, feeling along the legs as she went.

"OK, what you need to do is push the legs back in and turn the calf," Zane said, standing close behind her. Ellie began working the legs back in, working against the heifer's contractions. She kept up a silent, running prayer, and she breathed her thanks as she got the calf turned around.

When the front feet appeared, Zane helped Ellie pull. A moment later, a slippery little black calf lay on the thick hay at their feet.

As Zane grabbed the calf by the feet and pulled it away from the heifer, Ellie stripped the glove off her arm. Turning, she saw Zane was bent over the calf, cleaning out its nose and mouth. The calf shook its head, its ears flopping. Then it let out a little sound. Its skinny sides were heaving in and out as it sucked in air, and Ellie moved closer to Zane.

"It's fine," she told him, relief in her voice. "The calf's going to be fine."

"Step away, and I'll let the mama go," Zane told her.

He swung the panel open and released the head gate holding the heifer. With an anxious lowing sound, the heifer backed out, turned and sought her calf. Her large, rough tongue immediately began to finish the job that Zane had started.

"I'll put them in a stall in a minute," Zane said, "but it can wait."

Ellie shivered and realized she was wearing only a dirty T-shirt.

"You can wash over there," Zane said, pointing out a hydrant in the corner. Ellie pulled the handle up and quickly rinsed her hands and arms in the icy water. She dried with paper towels Zane offered then put them in the sack of trash he had secured against the wall.

"I'd like to take this shirt off and put my sweatshirt on," Ellie said.

"Sure." Zane nodded, and promptly turned his back. Ellie stripped off the filthy shirt, let it fall to the ground and slid her arms into the bulky sweatshirt. She pulled her coat on and zipped it up.

"Much warmer," she said as Zane turned around. She picked up the T-shirt, shook her head then stuck it in the trash as well.

She watched as Zane moved the heifer and calf into an empty stall nearby. In the hay, the calf stood for the first time on wobbly legs. The cow lowed anxiously and licked her baby again. Then the calf began to nurse.

"It's wonderful," Ellie said. The calving barn was

The Compromise

warm and comforting, the lights filling it with a yellow glow. Several of the other pens were occupied with large black cows lying protectively next to small black bundles in the hay.

"You were wonderful. Where did you learn to do that?" Zane asked.

"Here. I learned it here." Ellie leaned against a nearby panel, arms resting on one of the pipes, head on her arms.

"Here? What do you mean?"

Ellie looked at him in surprise. "You mean no one told you?"

"Told me what?"

"I grew up here," Ellie said simply. "For seventeen years I lived on this ranch. My grandpa built this calving barn. My dad and I built the meadow fence. I'm the youngest of four, so when my brothers went to college, I was Dad's main helper. He taught me how to pull calves like I did tonight, although, I'll admit that I've only done it once or twice before."

Zane was shocked. He had been prepared for many explanations, but the one she offered was unexpected.

"MacCready, of the Flying M," he said thoughtfully.

"Yes, that was our brand. Many calves wore that brand over the years, and I had hoped for many more. But that was not to be."

"How could you leave? How could you sell this place?"

"Prices were bad for several years in a row. With my brothers away at college, there was no one to help. Mom and I did what we could to help Dad, but things were going downhill fast. Mom and Dad finally decided to sell while we were still far enough ahead to get out with some money. In the end, we had enough to start over."

They fell silent, watching the mother with her calf. Zane pushed up his coat sleeve and checked his watch.

"It's time to check the herd again."

Ellie nodded, and without being asked, she followed him out the door into the night. The wind was still bitingly cold, and she felt it wake her. Zane led the way through the corrals and into the calving pasture.

"I left the pickup out here when I brought the heifer in," he said.

Without saying a word, Zane moved to walk on Ellie's right, placing his body between her and the wind to shelter her as best he could. A few minutes later, they reached the pickup. Ellie climbed in, colder than ever, and waited for the heater to blow warm air.

Meanwhile, Zane had his window rolled down and the spotlight thrust outside. Ellie snuggled down in her seat, bouncing as they drove over frozen cow chips in the darkness, remembering. It was so good to be home.

They circled the pasture, but all was quiet. Zane drove back to the yard and dropped Ellie off at her house. As she entered, she glanced at the clock on the wall. It was nearly four a.m. The only really good thing

The Compromise

about it was that tomorrow – today, actually – was Saturday. She could sleep in.

As she crawled back into bed, she decided that she was truly home again.

"Thanks, God," she whispered as her eyes closed. "Thanks for bringing me back to the ranch."

Chapter 8

"Ellie?" Zane called, knocking on her open front door.

"Just a minute." Ellie emerged from the kitchen, broom in hand. "Hi."

"Sweeping the steps?" Zane asked as he stepped aside to let her pass.

"Yep. They're filthy. That last snow left dirt everywhere when it melted." Ellie leaned on the broom. "I don't suppose you came by just to ask me that, though."

"No, I didn't. Actually, I have to go to Scottsbluff today and get some parts for the tractors. I was wondering if you needed anything. I'll be going to the grocery store and probably one of the big discount stores, too."

"It wouldn't be a bother?" Ellie asked, propping up the broom against the side of the house.

Zane grinned, his gray eyes lit up. "Now, Ellie, if it had been a bother, I wouldn't have stopped and asked in the first place, would I?"

"You have a point. All right, I'll make a list. Come on

The Compromise

in while I find a piece of paper and a pen."

Zane took a seat at the kitchen table and watched her.

"I need eggs, milk, chocolate bars and coffee," she told him.

"Should I be worried about what you eat?"

Ellie looked up, face innocent. "No, just about what I don't eat – vegetables, meat, bread – that sort of thing."

Zane laughed, and as he did so, he realized that he had laughed more with Ellie in the past two weeks than he had in the past two months, before he got to know her.

"As for other items," she continued, writing as she spoke, "I would love to have some things for school. I don't know how easy they'll be to find, but if it's not a problem, I'd like some award stickers, or ones with smiley faces on them, as well as a few packages of balloons and anything else that looks like it would work at an Easter party – streamers, plates, napkins, cups, plastic eggs. Could you get about five sacks of Easter candy? I'm planning on going to town next weekend, but if it snows – and it could – I don't want to disappoint the kids."

"Sure, I can get your Easter stuff. Any kind of candy in particular?"

"The good kind, nothing cheap," Ellie specified. "But no gum. I'm not cleaning carpets."

"Yes, ma'am." Zane doffed an imaginary hat and stood up.

"Just a minute." Ellie disappeared into the bedroom and returned, a bill clutched in her hand. "Here, use this, and if it takes more, I'll pay you back tonight."

"Yes, ma'am. Goodbye, and don't forget to hold down the fort, ma'am."

Ellie had to bite her lip to keep from smiling as she shooed him out the door. "You behave, Zane Redding, and drive safely," she called after him.

After his pickup left the yard and was lost to sight behind a hill, Ellie realized the ranch suddenly felt a lot lonelier. She laughed at her own foolishness and picked up her broom again. A Western meadowlark sat on the fence post across the yard, warbling his cheery tune.

"Yes, I know," Ellie said to it. "It's almost spring. April sneaked up on us unaware, and now Easter will be here before we know it."

The weeks of school had gone quickly. It seemed that just a few days ago she was teaching that first day. Now, everything was moving faster and faster as the end of school, just a month away, approached. Ellie had an Easter party and multiple tests to plan, and time was the one thing she never seemed to have enough of.

After lunch, she heard a vehicle pull into the yard. It was too early for Zane to be back. She moved to the kitchen window and looked out. An expensive car was parked in front of her house, and a man stepped out. He looked around the yard quickly, almost distastefully, then strode toward Ellie's door. She stepped away from

The Compromise

the window and moved to stand beside the front door, waiting for him to knock before she opened it.

"Hello. Might Mr. Redding be at home?" the man asked.

Ellie decided that the Western suit and lizard boots he wore must have cost as much as her monthly paycheck, and the man still didn't look Western. In fact, everything about him rubbed Ellie wrong.

"No, he's not, and he won't be home until late tonight, Mr. ..."

"Jones. Mr. Jones. I'm sorry to have missed Mr. Redding, but I can certainly speak to you, if you would be so kind as to relay a message."

Ellie nodded, not liking him at all.

"I represent a ... a man of business, one might say. Do you recognize the name?" Mr. Jones fished a card out of his expensive suit and handed it to Ellie. She recognized the name, and things began falling into place.

"Yes, I know who this is."

"Well, we're interested in adding Mr. Redding's ranch to the significant piece of land we've already purchased west of here. Part of Mr. Redding's land adjoins ours, and we believe it would make a fine addition. We're prepared to offer top dollar. If Mr. Redding is interested, he can reach me at the number on the card."

Ellie nodded, then thought of a question as the man turned away. "Mr. Jones?"

"Yes?"

"May I inquire as to what the land you have purchased is being used for?"

"Um, yes. We're raising buffalo."

"Oh. In that case, I sincerely doubt if Mr. Redding is interested. If he is, he'll call."

As the car drove away, Ellie looked at the card in her hand and thought about crushing it. But she knew she couldn't. The message was for Zane, and she would deliver it. However, she had a feeling that she would be delivering more than just a message.

"He can't lose the ranch," she said to herself as she closed the door firmly. "I can't watch him lose it. I can't watch it sell ... not again."

When Zane's headlights arced through her living room window at nine o'clock that night, Ellie was ready. She pulled on her coat, tucked the business card in her pocket and marched next door. Zane was unloading the pickup, and after they exchanged pleasantries, she helped him carry the bags into the house. When they were finished, he asked her to come in while he sorted out her groceries and things.

"Please ignore the piles," Zane said as he held the door for her. "Life's been crazy, and you sure can see it here."

Even though he had been to her house often, this was the first time Ellie had been back in the big house since

The Compromise

her return to the ranch. It hadn't changed much, she thought. But then, she hadn't really expected it to. The furniture was different, but the mess wasn't bad at all. In fact, it was clean except for a pile of outdoor clothes on the floor by the door and a pair of mittens hung over a chair to dry.

"Here you are," Zane said, handing her five plastic sacks. "I don't know if I did all right on the Easter things, but I hope so. You didn't have much change left, but I put it in the blue sack with the top tied, along with the receipts."

"Thanks, Zane. I'll go put this away, but may I come back in a bit? I need to talk to you about something."

"Sure."

Ellie returned fifteen minutes later to find Zane putting away the last of his groceries.

"Pull up a chair, and I'll make a pot of coffee," he said. Ellie took her coat off, chose the chair without the mittens and sat down at the battered kitchen table. Zane started the coffee then joined her at the table.

"All right, what's up?"

"A man came to see you today, a Mr. Jones, and he offered to buy the ranch." Ellie handed the business card to Zane and explained what had happened as clearly as she could.

"Yeah," Zane said when she finished. "He's been after me for weeks. I finally got to the point where I just shut the answering machine off."

"So you're not actually considering selling the ranch?"

A lump of fear and something else in her throat made Ellie's voice sound almost tearful.

"Ellie, this land and these cows are my life. I'd sooner cut off my arm than lose this place."

"I couldn't watch you lose it," Ellie confessed, "especially not to ... to this media mogul and his buffalo."

"Got something against buffalo?" Zane teased gently.

"No. But I love this ranch, Zane. I always have. But really, how are you doing? Will you make it through the year?"

"Yeah, I'll make it through the year. It's gonna be tight, but I'll make it. And if I don't, well ..."

Ellie met his gaze and felt the concern and weariness within him.

"I have some savings, and my teaching paycheck is more than I need. If you need it ..."

"I can't take your money, Ellie," Zane said firmly.

"What if we made the ranch a corporation or something? What if we tied it up legally so that it couldn't be sold immediately, so that no one could get their hands on it?"

"Ellie, you're worried about something that will never come to pass. Besides, who would want to get into the mess I've got here?"

"I would," Ellie said softly.

"I can't do that to you, Ellie. I can't tie you down here,

The Compromise

not like that. Besides, I don't know if I'm ready to give up a piece of my dream."

"Please. I don't want to take your dream. I would like to share it. It's still your ranch, Zane, and it always will be, but I don't want to see you lose it. Can't we compromise?"

The only sound in the kitchen for the next few minutes was the steady drip of the coffee maker. Ellie sat quietly as Zane considered what she had said. Finally he spoke.

"All right, Ellie, we can compromise. We can form some kind of partnership, with you as one-quarter or one-half owner. And if at any time I have the capital to repay your initial investment plus interest, then the ranch reverts to me with no strings attached."

"And what kind of say do I have while I'm partner?" Ellie asked.

Zane grinned briefly. "Let me get us some coffee and a couple of sheets of paper. If we're gonna make this work, we need to hammer out some things and get them written down before we go to a lawyer. Agreed?"

"Agreed."

As Zane grabbed the coffee mugs, Ellie couldn't help asking, "What made you change your mind?"

"Do you really want to know?"

Ellie nodded.

"All right, then. I got to thinking about all the things I had to buy today just to keep the equipment running.

I've got enough money in the bank to get through the year with the bare essentials, but if something goes wrong, I'm out of luck. Beyond that, though, I had a scare this morning with the tractor. If I die tomorrow, I don't want this place to go to someone who will just sell it for the money. You love it, and I wouldn't mind you ending up with it. Mom and Dad are pretty well set, and my sister is just a kid yet, so they don't really need or want this place. You, though, would make this place work."

Ellie didn't know whether to feel flattered or scared to death. She took the paper and pen he offered her, and reached for her coffee. It looked like a long night.

When they finished, Ellie returned to her house. She was thankful that church services didn't start until after lunch. She needed to catch up on her sleep, and more than that, she needed some thinking time.

"Are you sure you want to go through with this?" Zane asked three weeks later, before they met with attorney Jon Carlisle to finalize the details and make them legal.

"I'm sure. I've prayed and prayed, and this seems to be the direction God is leading me."

"Mr. Redding? Miss MacCready?" asked Mr. Carlisle, a tall, distinguished, older gentleman, as he stepped out of his office. "Won't you come in and have a seat?"

The Compromise

They entered, Ellie first then Zane. Settling into the deep, soft seats, Ellie glanced at Zane for courage, then looked up as Mr. Carlisle took a seat behind his desk.

"Since I received your letters and spoke with you over the phone, I've drawn up the papers. I'd like you both to read them very carefully. Feel free to discuss them with each other and with me. Here you go." He handed two clipboards across the desk and settled back with some reading of his own.

It took Zane and Ellie both a good twenty minutes to read through the papers. When they finished, they both looked up.

"Any questions?" Mr. Carlisle asked.

Ellie had none, but Zane did.

"Why did you include the paragraph about both of us contributing to the upkeep and daily running of the ranch, both physically and monetarily? Ellie doesn't need to do that."

"On the contrary, as a partner, Ellie ought to be out there. She needs to know what's going on, and since the ranch is still mostly yours, she needs to be contributing," Mr. Carlisle said.

He turned to Ellie. "You finish school in a week, don't you?"

"Yes," Ellie said.

"There will be branding to do, and soon haying season will start. There will be plenty of ways for Ellie to help.

"You're not getting any younger, Mr. Redding, and things aren't getting any easier. Besides, there's a higher risk of danger when you're out working by yourself. If you two can compromise and work together, this crazy scheme you've cooked up might just relieve some of the pressure. Give a little, Mr. Redding."

Zane nodded. "Are you OK with this, Ellie?"

"I am."

"Then let's sign the papers."

They went out to supper to celebrate, then Ellie handed Zane the keys to her car. She had noticed him watching her on the drive to town, and she wondered how long it had been since he'd driven something that was just plain fun.

"You really want me to drive home?" Zane asked, taking the keys and eyeing her car.

"Do you want to?" she asked.

Zane grinned. "Yeah, I sure do."

As he shifted up through the gears, he said, "I feel like one of those race car drivers."

"Not a lot of racing you can do on a tractor," Ellie teased.

The ride home went quickly as they discussed the coming summer and their plans. That night, they both managed to get to bed early.

The hills, bright-green and shining with the promise of new spring grass, were dark beneath the star-filled sky. During the night, the cold crept over the land and

The Compromise

the icy fingers of a killing frost bit into the tender grass, killing it before the sun's rays warmed the morning. Thus, Ellie and Zane's compromise began with a disaster that set the stage for summer.

Chapter 9

"This one's ours, Ellie," Zane said. He moved as a horse stepped between them. A long rope stretched from the saddle horn to the heels of a calf being pulled behind it.

"Let's do it," Ellie said as she moved with him, grabbing the rope close to the calf's heels. With the rope in one hand and the tail in the other, she moved in time with Zane, who had the calf's front legs. In one swift movement, they put the calf on the ground. Ellie sat down in the dirt, but she didn't have time to complain. She slipped the rope off the calf's heels and held the upper leg tightly. The lower leg was pinned to the ground under her riding boot. Zane had the calf's front leg bent back and his knee on the calf's neck.

"Heifer?" Zane asked, and Ellie nodded.

"Looks like things are backed up," Ellie said.

"Yeah. That's OK. This little gal isn't going anywhere."

What he said was true. The calf lay motionless on the ground. Ellie let her arms relax as she took a look

The Compromise

around the branding corral. At the far end of the makeshift enclosure, the cows and their unbranded calves milled and bawled.

Earlier that morning, Ellie, Zane and other ranchers from the area had helped Mike Snow round up his herd and drive them into the holding pens. Once that was done, Mike had moved his old pickup containing materials to brand and vaccinate the calves into the enclosure.

Zane and Ben Thomson had helped Mike set up the stove and get the fire going. When the irons were hot, the branding began. Mike asked three neighbors to rope the calves and drag them out to the wrestlers. Once the calf was on the ground, one of the older men burned Mike and Jenny's brand onto the calf's hip. At the same time, another man with the vaccine gun lifted the skin on the calf's neck and injected it. Then they moved on to the next calf.

The most unpleasant part of the job, at least in Ellie's eyes, was castrating the bull calves. But, it was necessary.

If a calf exhibited signs of sickness, Mike would examine and treat the animal while the wrestlers had it on the ground. When everything had been done – all in the space of about three minutes – the wrestlers would release it and move out of the way. The calf would trot off, seeking its mother.

Sometimes a calf would run back into the bunch of

unbranded cows and calves, but usually they were successfully deterred.

"That's a thoughtful look," Zane said, breaking Ellie's reverie. "How are your arms holding up?"

"Better than they were last week," Ellie said with a laugh. "I think I'm finally getting back in shape. When I was sixteen, I could work all day and never feel a thing. Now ... I must be getting old."

"Yeah. I can see the wrinkles and gray hair already." Zane teased as Ben Thomson arrived with a hot iron.

"Sorry about the wait," Ben said before he lowered the iron to the calf's hip. As the calf struggled and bawled, Ellie hung on tight.

"Don't worry about it. We were just taking a break," Zane said. A second later, another neighbor arrived with the vaccine gun. As the men moved to the next calf, Zane looked at Ellie. "Ready?"

"Sure."

As Zane stepped back, Ellie dragged the calf's heels around in a ninety-degree circle so the calf was facing the opening in the corral. As she released the heifer, the calf rose, bawled again and surged toward the already branded calves. Ellie didn't see where it ended up. She turned and saw another roper headed in her direction with another calf – a big one.

"Oh boy," she muttered as she reached for the rope to begin the process all over.

The Compromise

They finished branding just after noon. Zane helped Mike load the equipment into his pickup, while the other men loaded their horses into stock trailers and drove down the pasture road to Mike's house.

Ellie reached down to brush off her hands but could not find a clean spot on her jeans. She was covered in dirt and manure. Her only consolation was that the other wrestlers were just as dirty. She had a clean pair of jeans and a shirt in the pickup to change into before they went in for lunch.

"Ready?" Zane asked Ellie, as Mike started up the pickup.

"Yeah. I'm hungry enough to eat two or three plates of food."

"You're in luck, then. I'll bet Jenny and the other ladies have enough to feed an army."

"They'd better."

Zane and Ellie walked slowly from the corral to Zane's pickup and trailer. Their horses were busily cropping grass. Ellie caught up the reins, and Zane loaded the horses. When the trailer door was shut, they got in the pickup, and Zane drove to the house.

"Mike's grass doesn't look much better than ours," Zane said, looking at the barren hills.

"No, it doesn't," Ellie said, holding on to the door as they hit a particularly bad hole in the rutted pasture road.

They pulled into the yard and parked the pickup.

Ellie grabbed her clean clothes and headed for the house. As she entered, the smell of dinner overwhelmed her. Ellie removed her boots on the back porch and entered the kitchen.

Jenny and six other women were bustling about, mashing potatoes, stirring gravy and finishing the last-minute details of the dinner.

"May I use your bathroom?" Ellie asked Jenny on her way through.

Jenny looked Ellie up and down, then said with a sparkle in her eyes, "Let's just say that if you don't clean up, you won't be sitting at my dinner table."

"Yes, ma'am."

Ellie grinned. She could hear the men outside, teasing and joking as they lined up to wash in the basin Jenny had provided. Ellie washed her hands and quickly changed clothes, putting her dirty clothes in a plastic sack.

"Need any help?" she asked when she returned to the kitchen.

"You've done enough already," Jenny told her. "Will you eat inside with us or out with the men and the kids?"

"Inside," Ellie said.

"Then go get an iced tea or pop if you want and come rest a minute."

Ellie moved outside. Long tables were set up in the garage, and most of the men were sitting on folding

The Compromise

chairs, drinking tea or pop. Kids were running around on the lawn, playing a game that involved two balls, a Frisbee and lots of shouting.

Some of the women were carrying platters of food from the house to a makeshift buffet table along one side of the garage. Ellie dodged a ball and entered the garage. She selected a root beer, popped the top and took a drink.

"It wasn't too long ago that you was out there yourself," one of the older men observed from a nearby chair.

"That may be so, sir," Ellie said. "But you haven't changed a bit." She grinned at him. "How have you been?"

"Oh, fair to middlin'. I hear you're teachin' school now."

The conversation came to a halt as Jenny stepped into the garage, placed a platter of roast beef next to the mashed potatoes, and called, "Dinner!"

The children lined up, taking paper plates and silverware. Some of the kids were so small that their mothers went through the line with them. As the last of the children moved on, the men moved toward the food.

Ellie waited about twenty minutes and went through the line with the other women. She needn't have worried about a shortage of food, she saw, as she reached the long table and the deep freeze on which platters and bowls were piled. When she finally finished piling food on her plate, she went back inside and joined the other women at the dining room table. Ellie squeezed in beside Jenny, and after a brief, silent blessing, she began eating.

"Oh, Jenny, this is delicious."

"Save room for dessert," Jenny said. "Every woman here brought a pie, and each one is better than the last."

After dinner, Zane and Ellie went home, unsaddled the horses and turned them out to pasture. They caught up on ranching chores and fed the cows. As evening approached, Ellie went to her little house and headed straight for the shower. As the water poured over her head, she could smell the smoke from the branding all over again.

Feeling clean again, she dressed in a loose, flowing skirt and a soft knit shirt. She put a load of clothes in the washer and fixed herself a light supper.

It was nearly seven when she opened the front door to let a cool breeze blow through the screen door. Ellie sat down at the piano and began to play. Halfway through one of her favorite pieces, she heard a knock on the screen door. Glancing over, she saw Zane.

"Come in."

She didn't stop playing, but finished the piece as Zane entered and sat down in the rocker.

"That's pretty good," he said. "Do you know how to

The Compromise

play anything fun, though?"

"Fun? Chopin is fun."

"I meant, something with words," he said.

"Mmm ..." Ellie reached for a large song book and flipped it open. Her fingers moved easily across the keys, producing a gentle country-western waltz as she sang, "I was dancin' with my darlin' to the Tennessee Waltz, when an old friend I happened to see ..."

When she finished the song, Zane applauded, saying, "You have a really nice voice, Ellie. Why don't you sing more often?"

"Singing is more work than just playing. When I'm playing, I let my mind wander. When I'm singing, I have to concentrate more," Ellie said.

She closed the book and turned to face him. "So, to what do I owe the honor of your visit?"

"I brought you those seed catalogs you wanted to see," he said, moving across the room to hand them to her. Ellie looked down at the brightly colored photos of giant carrots, squash, green beans and fruit on the covers.

"If I make up a list of what I'd like to plant, would you go over it and add anything I missed?" she asked.

"Sure. Your idea of sharing a garden is a good one, although with my schedule, I'll probably not be much help."

"That's OK," Ellie said. "I'm not much help fixing machinery, so we'll call it even."

Jo Maseberg

"All right." Zane moved back to his seat in the rocker, looking a little uncomfortable. Ellie looked at him suspiciously.

"What is it?"

"What?" Zane glanced up.

"Is there something else you need to tell me?" Ellie asked.

"Actually, there is, but you look really tired. It can wait until tomorrow."

"I'm not that tired."

Zane nodded. "I have bad news. Remember when I told you that Mom usually comes down and cooks my branding dinner while Dad runs the vaccine gun?"

"Yes."

"Well, Mom's down with a nasty bronchial infection of some kind, so she won't be able to make it on Saturday. Dad doesn't want to leave her, so he won't be here either. I hate to ask you, but can you ... would you cook dinner?"

Ellie remembered the feast Jenny had prepared and mentally cringed. Eleven years ago, she would have said yes in a heartbeat. Eleven years ago, she could have put on a feed for a crowd of thirty without wincing. But now she was so used to cooking for one that she wondered if she could manage it. Looking at Zane's worried face, though, she knew she would have to.

"Sure. Your mom was going to bring a lot of the groceries with her, wasn't she?"

The Compromise

"Everything but the meat. I've got ham and roast beef in the freezer."

"I'll need to make a menu and go shopping. Can you figure up about how many I'll need to cook for? I just need an estimate, so I don't run short on anything."

An expression of enormous relief crossed Zane's face as he nodded and rose. "I already did. We can expect about twenty-five, counting the wives who will come. You might cook for thirty, just in case."

"All right. I'll work on a menu and run it past you before I go shopping."

"Thanks, Ellie. Thanks a lot."

Ellie just smiled. She waited until Zane had stepped off the porch and moved down the walk before she let the smile fade.

She moved to the kitchen and found a notebook and pen, then she reached for the phone. Pushing the first speed-dial button, she heard it ring. A soft female voice answered.

"Mom!" Ellie said. "I need some help."

Chapter 10

The late afternoon sun lay upon the floor, warm to the touch and eye. With the windows and the front door open, a cool breeze circled through the little house, welcome after the earlier heat. Ellie gave her chair a nudge and rocked gently, allowing her weary muscles to relax at last.

"How did it go, dear?" her mother asked.

Ellie shifted the phone to a more comfortable position before answering. "It went well, really well. Jenny, Laurie, and three other women helped in the kitchen, and the men came right on time, so nothing got cold and no one had to wait. We had more than enough food, too. Zane and I will be eating leftovers for days, and I put some in the freezer for dinners later on."

"What did you finally decide to have?"

"Oh, salad and raw veggies, pickles and olives, fruit salad and the acini de pepe-marshmallow salad. Then for the main course, roast beef, ham, mashed potatoes and gravy, homemade rolls, baked beans, green bean casserole and peas and carrots. Everybody brought pie,

The Compromise

and I had made a cake, just in case."

"I'm proud of you, Ellie. I knew you could do it if you put your mind to it."

"Thanks, Mom. Anyway, I'm glad we only have to do it once a year. I can't imagine cooking a meal like that twice."

"You always did like to be outside more than in, but aren't you glad I pinned you down and made you learn how to cook and sew and knit and crochet?"

"Yes, Mom, I'm glad." Ellie smiled, wishing her mother was in the same room instead of so far away.

"Well, I'd better go get your dad's supper on," her mother said. "He's looking hungry."

"Bye, Mom."

"Take care, and I'll talk to you soon."

Ellie heard the click as her mother disconnected, then sighed and pushed herself from the chair, moving across the room to hang up the phone. She'd barely seen Zane all day. He'd left the house right after she had arrived to start dinner, and the dinner itself had been so crazy that he'd stayed outside most of the time. She and the other women had cleaned up afterward, and Ellie had put the leftovers in his fridge and freezer. She had closed the door on the neat kitchen and returned to her own house for a break.

Pausing indecisively, she suddenly remembered Jenny's invitation and Jenny's news. Sliding her feet into the sandals near the door, she headed across the yard. Zane's back door was open. He was sitting at the kitchen table, and when he saw her through the screen door, he waved her in.

"Have a seat," he offered, gesturing to the kitchen chairs. Ellie sank gratefully into the chair opposite him. "You saved my neck today," he continued.

"Our necks," she corrected. "I'm part of this too, now."

He nodded. "Yeah, you are. Still, that was a meal to be proud of, and I thank you. Everybody went back for seconds."

"And we still have leftovers," Ellie said with a laugh. "That's OK, though. Anyway, I didn't come seeking praise. Jenny invited us to dinner – supper – tomorrow."

"You accepted?"

"Well, after her other news, I told her I would come only if she let me bring food or if I come early enough to help cook. She told me I could cook."

"What other news?"

Ellie grinned. "She and Mike are going to have a baby!"

"No!" Zane's chair legs hit the floor, and he found himself grinning back. "That's great. When did she find out?"

"A couple of days ago. She's been so tired lately that she made a doctor's appointment. She thought she was just really run down, but apparently that isn't the case."

The Compromise

"I bet they're excited."

"Jenny said that Mike hasn't come down to earth since she told him," Ellie confirmed.

They both fell into a thoughtful silence until finally Ellie pushed back her chair. "Well, I'd better quit pestering you and go home."

"Oh, you don't have to rush off," Zane said quickly. "Do you want to watch a movie or play a game or something? I should be working in the shop, but I'm tired, and I think we both need a break."

"A movie might be fun," Ellie said.

"I don't have anything new, but you can look at the shelf and see what I've got."

Zane rose and led the way into the living room. Ellie had never been any farther into Zane's house than the kitchen. As he opened the door to the living room, and she followed him, she saw that this room had changed since she'd seen it last.

The wallpaper was gone, replaced by clean, white walls with Western prints hanging on them. The floor, once cold tile, was now carpeted with a thick, smoky-blue carpet, and the fireplace had a new oak mantle above it. She liked the furniture, too. Three large, oak bookcases sat against three walls. Two overstuffed chairs and a sofa, all in shades of blue, surrounded a coffee table. Near the fireplace, a television and video-cassette player occupied a small stand.

"Here," Zane said, standing by one of the bookcases.

Jo Maseberg

Ellie bent to peer at the row of titles.

"A lot of Westerns," Ellie said.

"They were my uncle's. I have just a few of my own."

Ellie nodded, then pulled one from the row. "How about this one?"

"John Wayne and Maureen O'Hara? How can we lose?" As he moved across the room to put the tape in the VCR, Ellie glanced at the contents of the other shelves. What she saw surprised her.

Between worn paperback Westerns sat a row of classics, also well-worn from much reading.

"Chaucer, Shakespeare, Hawthorne, Melville." Ellie read the authors' names. "Are these yours?"

Zane looked up from the VCR, an embarrassed grin replacing his former look of concentration.

"Um, yeah. I minored in literature."

"You've got some titles here that I haven't read yet, but you're missing some that I do have. Maybe we could trade books."

"Sure. I'd like that."

As Ellie curled up on the sofa, and the movie started, she couldn't help but wonder about this new facet of Zane. When she had first met him, he had seemed to be just a simple rancher, but as she grew to know him, she was discovering that he was anything but. She wondered at the way she was beginning to feel about him.

He was her friend, she finally decided. She trusted him. He was the first man outside her family – other

The Compromise

than Mike – whom she had trusted in a very long time. She sighed and leaned back to watch the show.

"Well, it looks to me like we're all done," Jenny said, drying her hands. The dishwasher was running quietly and the sink was clean at last.

"That was a great meal," Ellie said, rubbing her back, "but it seems like all I do since I moved here is eat."

"I know the feeling." Jenny led the way to the living room. "Would you like to see the afghan I've started for the baby?"

"Love to. Where did Peter, Zane and Mike disappear to?"

"Peter's upstairs, and I think Mike said something about a walk." Jenny sank down into her favorite chair and reached for her basket of yarn. "I know Mike is worried about the drought."

Ellie sat on the floor beside Jenny's chair. "Zane is too, and so am I."

"God will provide."

"I hope so, Jenny. I hope so."

Mike and Zane were walking slowly west along the meadow fence. The sparse grass was green, but stunted. The dry hills were brown, and the lake was not as full as usual.

"It's bad, Mike," Zane said quietly. "I wish that Ellie wasn't here. She's got her heart set on making the ranch work, and I don't know if we can, even with the money she's invested."

"I'm worried about Jenny, too. With the baby on the way, she shouldn't be doing as much, and with our two ranches combined, I'm not going to be able to do all the work myself. I've been thinking about getting summer help, but the two guys I had in mind are already hired out."

"How much help do you need?"

"Well, if this hay ever turns into anything, I'll need help putting it up."

"Looks to me like your hay is further along than ours. I could come over and help you hay here first, then start my haying after we finish."

"Would you really? I'll pay you and Ellie, but I've really got to have the help."

Zane shook his head. "Now, I didn't say anything about Ellie."

"Why not?"

"Do you really think she's up to it?"

Mike stopped in his tracks, turning to face his friend. "Zane, that girl spent every summer on a tractor from the time she was big enough to reach the steering wheel. She's mowed, raked, swept and stacked, and I've seen her do it. She may be a little out of practice, but give her a refresher course, and she'll do fine."

The Compromise

"You're sure?"

"I promise. You have to stop underestimating her."

They started walking again, and Zane shook his head. "I keep being surprised by her. She's so much a lady, but she's also a rancher's daughter and a cowgirl in her own right."

"I'm going to offer some advice, and you can ignore it if you want to, but you'd do well to take it. If you're unsure of Ellie's abilities, talk to her. She knows her limits, and she'll be honest with you."

"All right. You don't think she'll be offended if I ask her if she can do something?"

"Nope. She'll probably just feel like you're giving her a fair shake."

"All right, I'll try it. Thanks."

"No problem. You just make sure you and she are here when we're ready to make hay."

"Will do."

The time for a talk with Ellie came the next morning as she and Zane began to plant the garden. Zane had plowed the large plot behind the houses the night before, after their visit at Mike and Jenny's. They carried the box full of seeds out, set it on the ground and laid hoes and shovels beside it.

"How do you think we should do this?" Zane asked as they gazed at the expanse of bare soil.

"Well, we could put the squash, pumpkins, zucchini and cucumbers on the east, then a few rows of corn. West of the corn, we could plant beans, then tomatoes, carrots, onions and lettuce, and last of all, the potatoes."

"Sounds like you've got it all figured out."

Ellie shrugged. "We did it that way once."

"Ellie, I ... um, just want to tell you how much I appreciate everything you've done. This garden is going to mean a lot of work for both of us, but especially for you, and I know that you'll be doing a lot with haying too."

Ellie reached for Zane's hand and squeezed it. "Thank you for giving me another summer on the ranch. I don't mind the work, not when I know I'm doing it for the good of something I love."

Zane nodded, still surprised by the touch of her hand.

"Now," Ellie said briskly, turning back to the garden, "let's get this thing planted."

In the end, they set the plot up like Ellie had suggested. With stakes and string, they made straight rows and mounds with the hoe, planting as they went. It was long past lunch time when they finished, but both felt a sense of accomplishment as they turned the sprinklers on and stood to one side.

"We'll have to water it everyday to get a crop," Zane said, brushing dirt from his hands.

"And hoe and fight the grasshoppers," Ellie said, laughing. "I think we can handle it, though."

The Compromise

"You must like to garden."

"I always did. I love to be outside, and I love to work with my hands. In spite of that, my favorite part of gardening is canning."

"Really? My mom cans some, but not much. I've canned a little bit these past few years but not a lot. This is the first year I've plowed the whole garden."

"Well, you just wait and see what I put up for this winter," Ellie told him, a sparkle in her eyes. "You'll eat better than you have in years."

"That's a promise you'd better keep," Zane said, "because I'm going to hold you to it."

They both laughed, the sound ringing through the empty yard and echoing from the dusty hills. Laughter was a luxury most couldn't afford, but Ellie realized that without it, she and Zane would both go crazy. She had no illusions, though. She knew what they were facing because she had faced it before. She just hoped that she and Zane would be able to hold together better than her own family had. Otherwise, she could lose the ranch again, and she would not let that happen. Not now, not after the miracle that had brought her home again.

"I will not lose you," she told the land silently, fiercely. "I will not."

But who could tell the future?

Chapter 11

The morning sun shone brightly on the hills – too brightly for Ellie's taste. But as she rode past the corner of the lake, she couldn't help admiring the images captured on the water's surface. A midmorning breeze was cool as it flowed into the cab of the pickup, and from where she sat, squeezed between Mike Snow and Zane Redding, Ellie enjoyed the air.

Mike slowed the pickup and turned onto the pasture road at the east end of the valley. When they pulled up to a gate, Zane jumped out and opened it. After Mike crossed the gate, he waited for Zane to close it and get back in the truck. Finally, the south valley came into view. Three tractors with mowers attached sat where they had been parked the evening before, facing the uncut expanse of grass.

Rolling down one more hill to the relative flat of the pasture near the meadow, Mike slowed the pickup, stopping in front of the meadow gate. Zane again opened the gate, and after Mike had driven through, he closed it. Mike stopped the pickup near the tractors.

The Compromise

When he turned the truck off, Ellie slid across the seat and out the door. She was eager to start work.

"Let's get the bars put in," Mike said. "Can you get yours, Ellie?"

"Sure can," she said, reaching into the back of the pickup. The tailgate had been removed to give easy access to the contents of the truck bed. Near the cab, a large tank with a pump held gas for the tractors. Behind the gas tank were toolboxes, rags, a five-gallon jug of water, spare parts, a crowbar and several containers of oil. The center of the pickup bed held the freshly sharpened sickle bars.

Ellie grabbed one and carried it to her tractor. She slid the long, flat bar into the mower, then connected an arm the size of a broom handle from the mower to the bar. When started, the sickle bar would move quickly back and forth, the sharpened blades cutting the grass as the tractor moved down the field.

"Got it?" Zane asked as he finished with his tractor.

"Yup."

"OK. I'll check your oil. How are you fixed for gas?"

"I filled up last night."

Ellie stood back and watched as the men finished readying the tractors. Then she turned and gazed thoughtfully at the hills. She could almost cry, they were so dry. In the distance, cattle grazed on sparse grass. Already the range was showing signs of abuse, but there was nothing that could be done to prevent it,

Jo Maseberg

nothing except to wait and pray.

"You're all set," Zane said from behind her, and she turned to find him waiting for her. His eyes were thoughtful, and she wondered, as she climbed up and removed the can covering her tractor's exhaust pipe, what he had been thinking.

Ellie was truly a ranch woman, Zane thought, as he watched her tuck the can that she removed from the exhaust pipe into the box on the side of the tractor. In a long-sleeve, blue-print Western shirt, jeans, boots and baseball cap, she looked capable and pretty. Her short auburn hair curled beneath the back of the cap and gleamed brightly in the sunlight. As he swung onto his own tractor and started it, Zane knew that once again he had almost underestimated Ellie. She could make hay with the best of them.

As soon as all three tractors were started, Mike put his in gear and drove in a small, slow circle until he was headed parallel to the meadow fence. Dropping the sickle bar to the ground, he engaged the mower and started down the field. Ellie drove to a strip of uncut grass and started her own mower, following Mike, and Zane followed Ellie.

As Zane began to mow, he kept the tractor straight, following the edge of the grass that Ellie had cut. A little too far to the left and he would only be cutting a

The Compromise

swath six or seven feet wide instead of almost nine; a little too far to the right and he would leave a strip of uncut grass between his and Ellie's swaths. He also watched the bar, making sure that the grass fell straight over it and that nothing caught the sickles and prevented them from cutting. In better years, he would have had to stop the tractor to clear clover from the bar or to remove nests, but not this year. The sickle chattered eagerly, cutting through the sparse grass effortlessly.

Reaching the first corner of the land, Zane swung the tractor to the right, raising the bar as he did so, then dropping it again to mow the strip of grass he had missed, before moving ahead again – making a perfect corner. Looking across the meadow, he saw that Mike was nearing the starting point – the first round complete. It would take all morning to finish mowing, and it would be little enough for their efforts, but every little bit helped.

After eating the dinner Jenny had fixed, the three returned to the hayfield to stack the hay from the day before. Ellie and Zane raked the hay into long windrows.

Compared to other years, the rows were few and far between. As Ellie bounced on the tractor, she thought of how a rancher's life revolved around hay. Hay was cut and put into stacks or bales in the summer. In the fall, it was moved to stack yards. In winter, a rancher put the hay on a hay sled or in a feeder and fed it to the cattle. In the spring, they finished feeding and waited for the grass in the meadows to grow, and the process would begin all over again.

"But this year there isn't enough," Ellie said aloud, her voice lost in the roar of the tractor and the wind.

She knew the facts, but she refused to dwell on them. Instead, she focused on the lemon scent of the cured hay and the feel of the breeze on her face. The sun beat down on her back through the thin fabric of her shirt, but she was used to it now. As she approached the end of a scraggly windrow, she reached for the lever to her right and eased it ahead, bringing the row of metal teeth up and releasing the hay that had been rolling around behind the tractor in front of the rake teeth. She dropped the teeth to the ground again as soon as she cleared the windrow.

Within the hour, Ellie and Zane finished raking, and Mike began sweeping the hay into piles. As Ellie climbed up to the hydra-fork platform of the stacker, she looked down at the meadow and the two men on tractors.

Mike pushed a load of hay up to the stacker before Ellie was settled on the platform seat.

"You ready yet?" he yelled from the sweep as he sat at the bottom of the ramp.

"Hang on!" Ellie yelled back, raising the head and

The Compromise

retracting the bars that had held it against the ramp. She lowered the head to the ground, and Mike pushed the load into the head. He backed away to get another load, and Ellie pulled the lever to bring the hay slowly up the long ramp to the top of the cage and tumble it in. After two more loads, Ellie used the hydra-fork to pack it, so the stack would be tight and stand straight without falling apart.

Across the meadow, Zane was scatter-raking behind Mike's sweep, collecting bits of hay and putting them into a windrow for Mike to pick up. Before they finished the stack, all the scatterings would be put into it.

It was almost four o'clock when they finished. Ellie moved the fork, gently rounding the top on the stack. She lifted the fork into the air and fastened the head to the slide. Mike opened the cage, swinging back the sides to clear the stack, then he pulled the stacker away with a tractor. Ellie lowered the hydra-fork, and Mike chained it to the inside of the cage and fastened the cage shut, so that the fork wouldn't bounce when he moved the stacker from this meadow to the next.

Ellie climbed down and met Mike at the tractor, where he handed her the water jug. Although the ice had long since melted, Ellie drank long and gratefully before handing the jug back. As he drank, she gestured toward the stack.

"I can't believe we spent all afternoon on one stack."

Mike lowered the jug and wiped his mouth with the

back of his hand. "I know. We usually get three to four stacks from this meadow. One year, we got six. I don't know which is worse, though, the drought, or the grasshoppers."

Ellie nodded. "Seems like the hoppers are flourishing."

As she finished speaking, Zane pulled his tractor and rake up, jumped down and joined them, taking the water jug without a word. Ellie worried about him. He'd always been trim, but since they'd started haying, he'd grown thinner. The hollows of his cheeks were deeper and his eyes seemed larger. She told herself that she would cook a good meal and invite Zane to supper.

Zane finally lowered the water jug. "You want me to rake around the stack?"

"No," Mike said, shaking his head. "We're moving everything to the next meadow and we don't have any way to haul it. Besides, it's just a little dab. We can get it when we move the stacks this fall."

Zane grinned. "All right. Guess I'd better get my rake switched around for the big move."

"I'll bring the pickup," Ellie volunteered. They had moved the equipment between meadows enough times that they had developed a system. They moved two tractors at a time and one person drove the pickup so they could return to the meadow and get the rest of the machinery. It would be late when they finished, Ellie knew, but she wasn't as tired as usual.

The Compromise

When Zane drove the pickup into the yard at six-thirty that night, Ellie said, "Hey, do you want to come over in about an hour and have supper with me?"

"Aren't you too tired to cook?"

"Naw, I'm just getting my second wind," she said with a smile. "Really, do say you'll come."

"All right. Thank you."

Ellie headed for the house, and as the back door closed behind her, she stripped off her boots and hat, leaving them at the door. In the kitchen, she washed her hands and put half a chicken on to fry before going to the bedroom. She took a quick shower, donned a sundress and returned to the kitchen. By the time Zane knocked on the back door, she had the table set and the chicken nearly done.

"Come in!" she called as she poured iced tea into two glasses.

Zane entered, and she saw that he, too, had showered and changed.

"Hi! It's almost done, if you want to just sit down and rest a minute."

He didn't protest. He sat watching as she moved about the kitchen. "There," she said, placing the plate of golden fried chicken on the table in front of him. "All done." As she took her seat, she glanced at him. "Will you bless the food?"

Jo Maseberg

He nodded and bowed his head. "Father, thank you for this meal, and bless the hands that prepared it. Thank you for the day we had and bless those who are not with us tonight. Amen."

How often had she heard her father pray a prayer like that? And now, her hands were the ones being blessed, and her food was being prayed over. She swallowed the lump in her throat and smiled as she looked up.

"Help yourself," she said.

"It looks delicious."

Zane returned her smile and scooped potato salad onto his plate then passed it to her. He reached for a piece of chicken and a roll. For a while, they ate in comfortable silence.

When she refilled the tea glasses, Ellie asked, "How long do you think it will be until we finish Mike's haying and start on ours?"

Zane shrugged. "I don't know. I'd guess we've got another week and a half, at least, maybe two, which would put it at the end of June or beginning of July. We're doing a little better than Mike, though. I've been checking our meadows, and I don't think we have the grasshopper problem that he does. His biggest problem is getting the hay up before the grasshoppers eat it all. We're just short on water."

"Speaking of grasshoppers," Ellie said, "when I was weeding this morning, I noticed that they are getting worse in the garden. Could we spray for that?"

The Compromise

"I'll do it tomorrow morning," Zane said.

"And don't we need to ride the summer range and put out salt and mineral soon?"

"Tomorrow."

Ellie grinned and teased him gently, "And when did you promise to provide popcorn and a movie?"

Zane groaned, "Tomorrow."

Tomorrow was Saturday, and their morning would be free. Mike didn't mow on Saturdays, because he did not stack on Sundays. Ellie was grateful for that, but it sounded as though she and Zane would be working harder on their morning off than on a regular morning helping Mike.

Soon they would be making hay in their own meadows. Working for Mike was fun, but she just didn't feel the sense of belonging that she used to feel making hay with her family. Haying always had been a family affair, and that's what made it fun.

"What's that faraway look in your eyes?" Zane asked.

"I was just thinking of how my family used to make hay. Mom and Mark raked, Dad and Robert ran the sweeps, and James and I made stacking a team event. We took turns with the mowing, and we always had so much fun."

Zane smiled. "It sounds like fun. I wish sometimes I could have had that kind of childhood," he said wistfully.

"I was lucky," Ellie said, "and very blessed." She

smiled brightly. "But you have me now, and we'll have fun, too."

Zane had a sudden vision of redheaded children and Ellie working with him as a team in the hayfield. Where had that come from? And why did he so desperately want it to be real?

Chapter 12

"Hey," Zane said, knocking on Ellie's screen door.

"Just a sec," she called from across the living room. "Bye, Mom. I'll call you later," she said, then hung up the phone and came to the door.

"Ready to go?" he asked as she pulled the front door shut behind her.

Ellie tucked a stray lock of hair behind her ear and pulled on a dark-blue baseball cap. "Yes. I was going to knock on your door ten minutes ago, but my mom called."

"How are your folks doing?"

"Oh, pretty good. Mom said they're about ready for a vacation from the metal shop, but other than that and the climbing temperature in southwestern Kansas, they're doing well."

Zane grinned and asked, "Did you tell her that this was our last day of haying for Mike?"

"You bet I did! I told her we planned on taking a short break and getting our equipment ready before starting on our own haying. She wished us luck."

The Compromise

They reached the pickup, got in and rolled down the windows. Already the sun was shining brightly, and the air was hot. Ellie could hardly believe that it was the first of July. As they drove toward the main road, she said as much to Zane.

"Really? Then the Fourth is only three days away," he said, downshifting and stopping the pickup on the hill where the gravel road and the main road intersected.

"Do you want to do anything special?" Ellie asked.

"Well, my mom and dad and I usually get together and do something. Sometimes they come here, but a lot of times I go home. Still, with the threat of fire, I'd feel a lot safer staying here this year. Maybe they could come down, and we could picnic or have dinner. What would you like to do?"

"You don't have to include me," Ellie told him. "I would like to meet your folks, though."

"I want to include you, and they want to meet you, too. We'll do something together, OK?"

"OK."

That evening, Mike handed Zane a check, shook his hand, and hugged Ellie. "Thanks a lot. I owe you more than I'll ever be able to repay."

"This is more than enough," Zane assured him. "Are you sure you didn't miscalculate?"

"We may not have grass, but we're doing OK financially. You two helped us out of a bind, and this is only fair," Mike assured them. "If you don't need all the money for operating expenses, go out and have dinner somewhere. Take a break – you've earned it."

Zane handed Ellie the check, and they started home, waving goodbye to Mike once more.

"You've had a look at the books," Zane said as he drove. "Will this help?"

"This and my teaching paycheck should see us through the winter if nothing really big goes wrong," Ellie said.

"Good!" Zane smiled, his whole face lighting up. "How about a celebration? Would you care to join me for pizza this evening?"

"Homemade or frozen?" Ellie asked.

"Frozen, but homemade by my mom – guaranteed delicious."

"Let me shower, and I'll be happy to join you for dinner."

A few minutes later, Zane pulled up in front of Ellie's house, and she leapt lightly to the ground, closing the door after her.

"Seven o'clock?" he asked through the open window.

"Seven," she repeated. As he pulled away from her yard, she walked swiftly up the walk and into the house. All in all, it had been a very good day. She stripped off her boots and socks then padded over to the phone. She had promised to call her mother. Dialing

The Compromise

the number from memory, she frowned as the phone rang five long rings, then the machine picked up.

"It's just Ellie, calling back," she said after the beep.

As she showered, she thought that it was strange that no one had answered the phone, but she dismissed the thought as she debated what to wear. After spending the bulk of her days in jeans and long-sleeve shirts, she was eager to wear something light and cool. But she wanted something pretty, something that would make Zane's gray eyes light up. She chose a pale-green skirt and a crisp, cream-colored, sleeveless top. After pulling on her sandals, she went outside and looked at the garden before heading to Zane's for supper.

Two days later, on July third, Ellie still hadn't heard from her mother. She also was unable to get in touch with her brother in Colorado, but that didn't worry her in the least. After working in the garden all morning, she decided to go see how Zane was doing in the shop before cooking lunch for both of them. As she dusted off her jeans and walked slowly across the yard, a glint of sunlight off glass caught her eye, and she turned, looking up the road at the dust cloud and the vehicle in front of it. For a moment, she just shook her head in disbelief, then she turned and ran toward the shop.

"Zane!" she shouted as she neared the open doors of the big metal building. "Zane!"

He met her at the door of the shop, wiping grease from his hands. "What's wrong, Ellie?"

"Nothing!" she told him, her green eyes shining. "Look!" She pointed to the road where a large, red pickup pulling a camper was slowly crossing the autogate into the yard.

"Somebody has the wrong place," Zane said, turning to drop the rag on the floor.

"No," Ellie said, reaching for his arm. "Somebody has the right place. That's my parents' pickup and camper."

"Your parents?" Zane asked, slightly incredulous.

"Yes. Will you come say hello?"

"You bet I will."

Together, they walked over to where the pickup had stopped in front of Ellie's house. As they neared it, Ellie broke into a run. She hugged her parents who waited by the pickup.

Approaching more slowly, Zane decided he liked what he saw. Ellie's father was a tall, strong man with graying hair and a weathered face. Her mother was petite, just over five feet tall, with the same auburn hair and smile that Ellie had. Both of Ellie's parents were wearing jeans and Western shirts, although her father wore lace-up work boots while her mother had on sandals.

"Zane," Ellie said as he drew near, "this is my mom, Grace, and my dad, Gene. Mom, Dad, this is Zane Redding."

The Compromise

"It's nice to meet you," Zane said, shaking Gene's hand, then Grace's.

"Nice to meet you, too," Gene said, his expression friendly, his handshake warm. "Ellie's told us a lot about you, and about what you've done with the ranch."

"Looks like you're having a worse year than Ellie led us to believe, though," Grace chimed in, shooting her daughter a reproving glance.

Before Ellie could reply, another vehicle drove into the yard and stopped near the MacCready's pickup. It was a new, forest-green sport-utility vehicle with tinted windows. The doors opened, and two men jumped out.

"James! Robert!" Ellie hugged them both, dwarfed by their height. "What are you doing here? Rob, where's Sarah and the kids?"

"Whoa, little sister," James said, tousling her hair. "Calm down. We'll answer questions one at a time."

"All right then," Ellie said, punching him lightly on the arm. "Answer."

Robert was the one who responded. "Mom called us on the first and said that you were having a pretty tough time of it. She and Dad had decided to come help you hay. Jim here got the bright idea that he wouldn't mind coming along, and since Sarah and the kids were going to go visit her mother and abandon me in L.A. anyway, I decided to fly into Denver and come with him. Mark will be along in the morning; he and Annie decided to drive down from Montana."

"The whole family will be here?" Ellie asked, delight mixed with disbelief.

"If it's all right with Zane," her mother said.

Zane, having been temporarily forgotten by the group, was suddenly the center of attention. He looked from the two women with matching auburn hair to the three men, all tall and in excellent physical condition, the younger two with dark, curly hair.

"You're welcome to stay. I can put some of the bedrooms in the big house to rights and ..."

"Don't worry about it," Grace said, her smile warm. "Gene and I have the camper to stay in, and Rob and James brought their camping equipment."

James nodded. "I've got two four-person tents and enough cots and sleeping bags for the whole gang, just in case anyone wants to enjoy a warm, summer night in Ellie's back yard with us."

"How long can you stay?" Ellie asked, looking at her family.

"Two weeks," her father said. "And consider this a working vacation. We're here to help with haying."

Zane watched in awe as Ellie's mother had her three children haul sacks of groceries into Ellie's house. Somehow, he ended up in the queue as well and found his arms full.

"Just set them on the floor," Ellie told him as she started emptying sacks into cupboards and the refrigerator.

The Compromise

"Your folks don't do things by halves," Zane said cryptically as he ducked out of Robert's way and headed for the camper once more.

"Tell Mom to come help cook!" Ellie called after him as she emptied a third sack. Even the prospect of cooking for seven people for two weeks did not wipe the smile off her face.

After a quick lunch of beans, hamburgers and chips, Ellie and her mother cleaned up the kitchen then spent the rest of the afternoon in the garden. Ellie's father and brothers helped Zane ready haying equipment in the shop, and everyone, Zane included, shared a delicious supper.

After dark, Zane went home, and Ellie's family began to prepare for bed. Finding the linen closet painfully short on towels, Ellie went next door and knocked. Zane opened the door, looking tired.

"I hate to bother you, but do you by chance have some extra towels? I think I'm short by three."

Zane nodded, then turned to lead the way.

"You're in luck. My mom thinks my dryer eats towels, so she gets me a new set once or twice a year. I've got a shelf full of brand new ones. You're welcome to as many as you want."

He opened the closet door and pulled out a pile of towels in shades of blue, then added washcloths and hand towels. Ellie could barely see over the pile. Seeing her plight, Zane removed half the pile from her arms and nodded toward the door.

"I'd better walk you home, or you'll trip on something in the dark."

Ellie smiled. "All right. I appreciate the loan and the help too."

As they stepped out of the house into the darkness, Ellie could hear her brothers' voices and saw the lights in her parents' camper.

"They don't have to sleep in the yard," Zane said suddenly. "I've got extra rooms. I don't have extra beds, but the floor beats the ground any day. For that matter, tell the guys they can come use my bathroom, too."

"Thanks, Zane, but I think we'll be OK." Ellie fell silent for a moment, then stopped so suddenly that Zane was several steps away before he turned back. They were almost exactly halfway between his house and hers, and the night was darkest there.

"What is it?" he asked.

"Are you OK with this invasion? I mean, really OK?"

Zane paused, then answered thoughtfully, "Yeah, I am. It kind of surprised me at first, but after working with your dad and your brothers this afternoon, all I can really say is that I appreciate the help."

"Everything went well, then?"

"Yeah, but I have a question for you."

"Shoot."

The Compromise

"Can you tell me about your brothers and what they do? I've tried to put some things together from what they've said, but I'm at a loss."

Ellie chuckled softly. "I guess I didn't even think about that. Do you know which one is Robert and which one is James?"

"Yeah, I have that much down."

"OK. Robert is the oldest – he's thirty-five, but don't tell him that I told you. He's married to Sarah, and they have two kids, a boy and a girl. They live in California, and Robert is a corporate executive for one of the big computer-chip manufacturers. You haven't met Mark yet, but he's coming tomorrow. He's thirty-three, and he recently married Annie, who's a really sweet person. They live in Montana, and Mark teaches college geology. Annie teaches history at the same place. James is single and lives in Colorado. He's thirty, and he's an engineer – numbers, not trains."

"And you're the youngest?"

"Yes, I'm twenty-eight."

"Only a year younger than me," Zane said.

"Really?" Ellie shifted the towels in her arms, then asked a question of her own. "Your family is still coming tomorrow for the Fourth, right?"

"Oh! I forgot all about that," Zane said softly. "Yeah, I guess they'll be here before lunch. Mom's bringing salad and dessert."

"You just have one sister, right?"

"Mmm hmm. Sheila's twenty, a junior in college and far too serious for Mom's comfort. She acts like she's forty."

"And your mom's a nurse, and your dad's a vet?"

"Right."

Ellie started walking again. "I just hope the whole gang gets along tomorrow."

"They should. You and I get along, don't we?"

"We do, don't we!"

They had reached Ellie's door. Zane added the rest of the towels to the pile in her arms and smiled at her in the light cast by the living room window. "Good night, Ellie."

"Good night, Zane. Sleep well."

As he walked away into the darkness once more, she stood motionless on the step, looking after him. In so many ways, Zane was the man she had dreamt of since high school. He loved the ranch – her ranch. They read the same things, they could talk about anything and they worked well together. Beyond that, she had become attached to the tall, lithe cowboy in a way that she hadn't even noticed until now.

"I want my family to like you. And more than that, I want you to like them," she whispered into the night.

Overall, everyone seemed to have hit it off. It was hard to tell, though. Her family was in shock. They never expected to find themselves back on their old ranch.

The Compromise

Ellie shook her head and turned to mount the porch steps. This new feeling she had for Zane would need sorting out, but everything was too busy now. After her family left, there would be time to think. For what, after all, was love? Was it this quickening of the heart, this eagerness of the eyes to just catch a glimpse of him? Or should there be something more, something deeper and intangible? How, after all, did one know what was love, and what was not?

In the dark outside the camper door, Ellie's father watched her thoughtfully. After a moment, he reached up and opened the camper door. "Honey? Ellie has more towels."

"I'm coming."

As Grace stepped down from the camper, she touched her husband's shoulder. "Why are you looking so solemn?"

He kissed her cheek, saying, "I'll tell you later."

"You'd better," she said saucily, then she headed for the house.

Ellie's dad knew how Ellie felt about Zane. The question was, how did Zane feel about her?

Chapter 13

The adage about too many cooks spoiling the broth couldn't be more wrong, Ellie mused on the Fourth of July, as she turned chicken in one skillet, her mom checked more in another and Clara Redding, Zane's mother, replaced the lid on a third pan.

At the kitchen counter, Sheila, Zane's sister, put relish items in small glass dishes, nibbling her favorites as she did so. Outside, the banter of the men drifted across the lawn and through the open kitchen window.

"This looks great," Ellie said as she turned one last chicken leg and set the lid back on the skillet.

"It smells even better," Sheila said, and Ellie smiled, turning to look at the young woman. Sheila was almost as tall as Zane. Her light-brown hair was a shade darker than his. She was majoring in math and had the lithe, stylish figure of a fashion model and the same easy grace. She made friends easily, with her sweet smile and hazel eyes that twinkled when she laughed. Ellie liked her the moment they met.

Just as Ellie and Sheila had become friends, so had

The Compromise

their mothers. Even though they just met, Clara Redding and Grace MacCready moved about the kitchen working with the ease of lifelong friends. Tall, blond Clara and petite, auburn-haired Grace were quite a pair, Ellie thought to herself; she only hoped that she would age as well and as gracefully as her mother.

"Go check the progress of the men, Ellie dear," Grace said, taking the fork from her daughter.

"Sure," Ellie said sorrowfully, "send me out to monitor the ruffians."

"I'll come provide moral support," Sheila said as she popped an olive in her mouth.

"Offer accepted," Ellie said quickly, smiling. "Let's go check."

"Look up the road and see if there's any sign of Mark and Annie," Grace called as they left. "They promised to be here in time for lunch."

"Maybe he forgot how to get here," Ellie said.

As the back-porch screen door creaked shut behind them, Ellie and Sheila surveyed the men and their project from the top of the steps. The spreading cottonwood trees shaded the sprawling lawn. Zane, Robert and James were actively engaged in finding a level spot on which to set one of the long tables that had been used during branding season. Folding chairs were leaned against the trees, waiting. Beneath the rustling leaves and towering trunks and branches, Ellie's and Zane's dads sat in lawn chairs overseeing the operation. The women watched as Zane and Robert lifted the table once again and shifted it in James' direction.

"Set it down right ... there," James directed, eyeing the legs of the table. "Now, does it wobble?"

Robert gave it a tentative push. Zane was less circumspect. The table did, indeed, wobble.

From her vantage point on the back steps, Ellie thought the table was perfectly centered. It sat in the exact center of a ring of cottonwood trees, completely shaded and on an almost flat part of the lawn.

"It looks good, guys!" she yelled as they reached to shift it once again.

"Yeah, but it rocks!" James said.

"So stick something under one of the legs," Sheila offered. "Then set up the chairs, and Ellie and I will set the table, so we can eat."

"A shim!" James exclaimed. "Now why didn't I think of that?"

"Maybe it's because you weren't the one moving the table," Robert said dryly.

In his lawn chair, Gene MacCready rolled his eyes and shook his head. "They can build supercomputers and skyscrapers, but give them a simple task and just see what happens."

Marshal Redding, known to the owners of his animal patients as Doc Redding, nodded his head in agreement. "I think they all need a refresher course in logic."

Ellie and Sheila laughed, then ducked back into the

The Compromise

house to get the tablecloths and dishes. When they stepped out once more, a car was pulling into the yard. The men abandoned the table and chairs to greet the latecomers.

"Go on," Sheila said, taking the dishes from Ellie's arms. "You haven't seen him in a year. I'll set the table."

Ellie squeezed Sheila's hand gratefully, then ran for the car, yelling into the kitchen window on her way, "Mark's here!"

When the car door opened, and a lanky young man in jeans and a neat polo shirt stepped out, Ellie hugged him tightly.

"Hey, now," Mark protested, then he grinned and hugged her back. "How are you, little sister?"

"Better than ever." Ellie stepped back and eyed him carefully. "You certainly look good. Married life must agree with you."

"I keep telling him that," said a petite blonde stepping out of the passenger side of the car. "But he always claims that it's the teaching, not the wife."

"Well, they both keep me on my toes," Mark said, ducking as a travel pillow sailed through the air toward him.

Ellie caught the pillow and returned it to the car. "Whatever it is, it's good to see you, Mark, and it's good to see you, too, Annie."

"Thanks, Ellie." Annie smiled graciously and returned the hug Ellie gave her.

As Robert and James joined them and hugged Annie, they teased Mark about his ability to arrive just before lunch, after all the work was done.

Watching the four siblings together, Zane wondered what he and Sheila had missed. They were close, but not as close as the four gathered around the car from Montana.

"They're a tight family, aren't they," Sheila said at Zane's side.

He glanced over at her. "Do you wish we had two more siblings, Sheila?"

"Not on your life!" Sheila retorted, then laughed. "I'm just wishing that one of those men was a little younger and a lot more interested in tall brunettes."

Zane was wishing something along those same lines, but the object of his hopes had red hair and green eyes.

After both families had eaten, they sat talking and laughing at the dinner table.

"So you all just came on the spur of the moment to help with haying?" Zane's father asked from one end of the table.

"In one way or another," Gene MacCready said. "I don't fancy bouncing around the field on one of those old tractors, but I'll keep 'em running and work in the shop. I know Ma doesn't want to get out there either, but she came prepared to cook and garden."

The Compromise

"I almost wish we could stay and watch," Zane's mother said.

"I have to go home and mind the animals, Mother," Marshal Redding said.

Sheila looked up from her place midway down the table. "Can't I stay for a while, Dad? That is, if they'll have me. The next two weeks are free for me."

"Do you want her?" Marshal asked, looking at Zane and Ellie.

"I don't mind if Zane doesn't," Ellie responded.

Zane agreed, saying, "Stay, Sheila. I've been trying to make a rancher out of you for years, and now I finally get my chance."

That evening, after Zane's parents left, Ellie drifted through the house, asking if anyone wanted more iced tea. Zane was playing pinochle with her parents and Robert at the card table. On the front steps, Mark waited impatiently for Annie to tie her shoes so he could take her on a tour of the place where he'd grown up. In the kitchen, Sheila and James were working on a complicated math problem involving stress, strain and some unidentifiable load.

Taking a seat on the deserted back steps, Ellie leaned against the house and sighed. She couldn't remember when she'd been happier. Through the open windows, she heard laughter, then Zane said, "Table talk is

Jo Maseberg

against the rules! Rob, deal again."

Ellie chuckled softly to herself. She had been worried at first that Zane would be shy around her boisterous family, but he was fitting in just like another brother. He had opened his home and his heart to her family, and she knew that she would never be able to thank him enough.

She knew that coming back to the hills had been at once a blessing and a curse.

This place grows on you, Ellie admitted to herself. She had told Zane at the beginning of their compromise that she could move on, that she could relinquish her hold on the ranch, but that had been a lie. Admitting it to herself brought an uncomfortable thought to light. Did she like Zane for himself, or was she subconsciously trying to get the ranch?

"Admit it, Ellie," she said to herself, "if you marry Zane, it's all yours."

The thought scared her. Less than twenty-four hours ago, she had admitted to herself that she liked Zane in a way that went beyond friendship. Now she was questioning her motives.

When Mom told me today how hard it was for her to come back, then told me how much she admired me because I came back to live, knowing I would have to leave eventually, I brushed it off. I didn't contemplate leaving then, and I don't contemplate it now. I want to stay here forever. Will I do anything to stay?

The Compromise

As the night grew dark, Ellie knew it was time to go to bed. The group had agreed to call it quits around ten. As she entered the kitchen, she saw that Sheila and James had finished the equation and were discussing the merits of their answer – Sheila arguing for more beams and James arguing for increasing the strength of the original number.

"Almost time for bed, you guys," she said, dropping a hand to her brother's shoulder.

"All right, Ellie."

Everyone knew they had a busy two weeks ahead of them. As much fun as it was to visit, they had time enough for that later.

The next morning, Ellie's brothers checked out the tractors, while Ellie and Zane stood talking with her father.

"You don't have much hay, but if we can run the two mowers all day, then operate the stacking crew behind them, we could get a lot of land covered," Gene said.

"Do you think we can keep them fixed and running for that length of time?" Zane asked.

"You're a good mechanic, Zane, and I'm not half bad. I think we can do it."

"We'll have to take turns on the mowers, and when it comes time to stack, we've got two rakes and two sweeps, as well as the stacker."

"Let's rotate people so nobody gets bored. Who do you think should start mowing?" Gene asked.

"Well, since Ellie knows the ropes, she and one of her brothers can start. Then you, me and the other two guys can get the rest of the equipment tuned up and in the field."

Within an hour, Ellie and James were on the mowers cutting the first of three hay meadows. After lunch, Zane and Mark took over and continued to mow all afternoon.

The following afternoon, Ellie and Sheila were seated on the stacker, watching Mark and Annie – herself a ranch girl from Montana – mow the far end of the meadow. Closer, Rob and James were raking, and Zane and Gene were sweeping. Ellie was hard put to keep the stacker head empty and the growing stack evenly packed.

"This is awesome, Ellie," Sheila said as they set the stacker up for a second stack.

"You're not bored yet?"

"Nope. I could watch the straight rakes forever. I don't know how the guys do it, but every time they get near a fence, they swing the rakes around, just miss the wires and posts, and somehow end up turned in the other direction to drop the hay on the windrow."

"Here comes one of the rakers now," Ellie said with a laugh.

James stopped the old, green tractor fifteen feet away

The Compromise

from the stacker and jumped down from the hot, metal-and-vinyl seat. As he reached the stacker, he grabbed the water jug and took a long drink. Looking up at the two women, he waved, then yelled, "Sheila, you want to ride on the rake for a while?"

"Could I?"

"Sure!"

Ellie watched as James climbed onto the tractor, then gestured for Sheila to climb up and stand beside the seat, holding onto the back of the seat and the left fender. As the tractor moved down the field, Ellie could see James pointing at the various levers and knobs. Then Zane brought the first sweep in, and Ellie went to work.

The next chance she had to check on James and Sheila came more than an hour later. At the far end of the meadow, she could see that Sheila was raking by herself. The rows were a little crooked, but she was getting the job done. Ellie saw that James was switching places with her dad on the sweep. As she watched, her father began walking toward the house and workshop.

At the end of the afternoon, they had completed a respectable three stacks. For the amount of meadow cut, however, three stacks weren't enough. Still, Ellie felt a sense of accomplishment. As the equipment was pulled away from the last stack and parked, Ellie, James, Mark, Annie and Sheila piled into the back of Zane's pickup. Zane and Robert got in the front and headed for the house.

Ellie turned her face into the summer breeze and gripped the sides of the pickup, praying silently, "Thank you, God, for bringing us home and together again. Thank you for so many things."

Each day passed in a similar fashion, with the evenings full of laughter and games. On Sunday, Ellie watched her family file into their old pew at church. That night, she took a quiet walk by herself. Upon her return, she walked to the shop to see why the lights were on. Zane was the only occupant.

"Hi," he greeted her, unplugging an extension cord from an outlet above the workbench.

"What are you doing?" Ellie asked, sticking her hands in her pockets.

"Just getting something ready for tomorrow. But I'm done now. Will you take a walk with me?"

"Sure."

Ellie waited outside, trying to ignore the beating of her heart and the lightness in her soul, as Zane shut the lights off and closed the big sliding doors. Together, they walked toward Ellie's house.

"Sounds like they're at it again," Zane said as they grew near. "I hate to say it, but your folks table-talk worse than a pair of kids. It sounds like Mark and Annie are doing the same thing just to keep even."

"Looks like Rob's still on the phone with Sarah and

The Compromise

the kids," Ellie said as they turned onto her walk. She could see her brother clearly through the open curtains.

"Where's Sheila and James?"

"Same place as usual," Ellie said. "He's about got her talked into getting a degree in engineering."

"Is it just me, or ..." Zane's voice trailed off. "Never mind."

"No, don't do that. Tell me what you were going to say."

Zane took a deep breath and leaned against the post of the porch. "Seems like Sheila and James are spendin' a lot of time together."

"I've noticed, too, but Mom and Dad aren't worried."

"Guess I shouldn't be either. She's probably just having fun because she's able to talk to someone who understands what she likes and why she likes it."

"If he wasn't ten years older than her, they'd be a good match," Ellie said quietly.

"Ten years isn't so much. My grandparents were twelve years apart."

"Ten years may not be, but she's still in college, and he's got a career in Colorado. They both have plenty of chances to meet other people, and who knows if they'll ever meet each other again?"

They were silent for a time, then Zane said quietly, "What if they're meant to be together? How do they know?"

"How does anyone know?" Ellie asked. "I guess a lot

of prayer is in order – and a lot of thinking."

"Good advice," Zane said, and went in to get Sheila.

Something in his voice made Ellie look after him. The way he had said good advice and the sigh that followed almost had her believing that he wasn't talking about a hypothetical situation. She shook her head and followed him. It was late, and they would be back at work the next morning.

Chapter 14

A week later, haying was over and all the company had gone home. The ranch felt empty, and as Ellie worked in the garden, she found herself looking up frequently – for what, she didn't know. She had learned to live alone happily, but after two weeks with family around, life seemed empty. In addition, the drought was pressing down, and fire was a real danger.

Almost every rancher had a firetruck – some were just pickups, with enclosed tanks of water in the back and equipped with fireproof suits and helmets. When a fire was sighted, all the ranchers responded. Zane was no exception. He had called Ellie on several occasions before leaving in the middle of the night to tell her where the fire was. Often, Ellie sat up and waited for him to return; sometimes she called Jenny to ask what she knew.

The local ranchers had been lucky so far; no one had suffered massive destruction. The worst fire scares were those emanating from a large wildlife refuge to the southwest. The land there had been left to the forces of

The Compromise

nature and the dead grass could easily catch fire. Fires were allowed to run rampant there, but fire failed to respect property boundaries, and if a refuge fire escaped, it could bring heartache and tears to more than one rancher.

During the nights when Zane did not return before dawn, he was usually helping put out a refuge fire. Sometimes he had to sit and wait for the fire to cross the boundary. When he did come in, Ellie would cook him breakfast then send him to bed to catch up on his sleep. With the haying done, they had only to ride the summer range, put out salt and mineral, oil the windmills, and check for sick animals. Zane also checked the fences for broken posts or downed wires. Ellie's days revolved around the garden, where she had more than enough time to think.

The more time she spent on the ranch, whether it was in the garden or in the pickup riding the summer range, the more she fell in love with her old home. She had always been a spiritual person, attending church regularly, reading her Bible and praying. But coming back to the place where God had become real to her as a child brought her faith to a new awareness. She found herself stopping to stare in amazement and praise God for the tiniest things – a butterfly, a clear, blue sky, clouds, a hill of grazing cattle or a sunset.

"Help me, God," she prayed, "help me know my heart. What is love? Is what I feel for Zane the real thing, or am I using him to get the ranch back?"

The answer was slow in coming, and her feelings were growing daily. Zane, wonderful Zane with his captivating gray eyes and sweet smile, showed no sign of feeling something more for her. Although, she sometimes thought his hand lingered on her arm a second longer, or his smile seemed a fraction sweeter. But that could be the anxious imagining of a hopeful heart. As it was, she struggled with her own mixed emotions – the most noticeable one was guilt.

At the end of July, the green beans were ready to be picked. Ellie took a dishpan and began to crawl along the rows, picking beans. With three long rows of beans, she had more than enough to keep her busy. If hay was in short supply, beans were not. When she finished, she had two dishpans and a turkey roaster full of them.

Lugging them into the house, she washed her hands, changed into shorts and a T-shirt and made lunch. After washing the dishes, she popped an audiotape in the player, turned up the volume and began to snap beans. She finished snapping three hours later, just as the tape ended. She dumped half the beans into the clean sink and covered them with cold water. Rinsing them a handful at a time, she put the clean ones into a clean dishpan. When all the beans were washed, she began the long process of canning.

The Compromise

It was after five when Zane knocked and entered. Ellie was emptying the canner for the second time, and the kitchen, despite the open windows, was hot with steam and smelled of green beans.

"You're making progress," he said, as she placed the last pint on the table and flipped a towel over it.

"One more canner load. I'm cooking the rest for supper."

"How many pints do you have?"

"Umm," Ellie paused before her list on the refrigerator door. "If all the jars seal, I have eighteen pints done and another nine to go. That makes twenty-seven."

"A month of green beans, at a pint a day," Zane said, rolling up his sleeves. "How can I help?"

"Are you serious?" she asked.

"You bet."

Ellie turned and picked up a container full of bean ends and sand. "How would you like to haul this out to the compost pile?"

"I can do that."

She watched him go, shook her head and turned back to finish filling the canner. When he returned, the canner was on the stove, beginning to boil. Ellie had put the canning supplies back in the cupboard and was washing the dishpans and turkey roaster.

"Would you care to join me for supper?" she asked, as he slid the empty container into the dishwater.

"Are you sure?"

"Yep. We'll be having fresh beans with green onions, hamburgers and macaroni salad."

That evening, after Zane returned home and the canning was done, Ellie drove over to the school in the valley. Using her key, she entered the building and filled several boxes with teacher's editions on every subject and grade level that she would be teaching. She put the boxes in the trunk and drove home.

Ellie took the boxes into the living room. Several contained spelling and vocabulary books that she had ordered earlier in the summer. She also had ordered new social-studies books.

Ellie arranged the books in piles by grade then grabbed a notebook and a pen and began outlining ideas for interdisciplinary units. Before school started, she hoped to have the units typed up and put in a three-ring notebook with worksheets, page assignments, and tests figured in. Her office file cabinet contained several grade levels of material from previous years; it was just a matter of sifting through files and locating the projects she wanted.

It was late when she finally called it quits and went to bed. Less than two hours later, the telephone interrupted her sleep. She grabbed the receiver.

"Hello?"

"Ellie, it's Zane. There's a fire."

The Compromise

The words pulled her to alertness.

"Where?"

"On the refuge, and it's headed this way."

"Can it be stopped?"

"I think so. But if you smell smoke coming over the hill, I want you to get in your car and get out of here, you hear?"

"I hear." Ellie paused, "Zane ... be careful."

She could almost hear his smile. "I will. 'Bye."

"'Bye."

Ellie hung up the phone and swung out of bed, unable to sleep. She worried about Zane going into harm's way once again. She padded silently out to the front room and stared out the window, watching Zane's flashlight bob, as he headed down the slope to the firetruck. It roared to life, the sound of the engine shattering the silence. As Zane drove the lumbering beast from the yard, Ellie bit her lip and prayed with all her might that he would return safely.

For a long time, she stood at the window. Finally, the long day began to catch up with her, and she took a seat in the glider rocker, gently rocking until she fell asleep.

The sun was high in the sky when Ellie awoke. She looked at the clock. Then, still in her pajamas, she ran outside to see if the firetruck was parked in its spot.

It wasn't there.

Ellie ran back inside, slipped her feet into sandals, and canvassed the ranch from the barn and the corrals past her house and garden, to Zane's house. She went to the shop and the stack yard, all the while yelling for Zane. Returning home, out of breath and near panic, she gripped the top rail of the porch, trying to think.

Mike!

She walked to the phone and dialed Mike and Jenny's number.

"Jenny? This is Ellie. Is Mike home from the fire? May I speak with him?" She waited, trying to breathe normally. "Mike? When did you last see Zane? He was on his way home at seven? You're sure? Where were you guys? No, I'll go look. I'll take my cell phone, and if I don't find him, I'll call. Get some rest, and thanks."

Ellie hung up the phone and grabbed her car keys and cell phone on the way out the door. Sliding into the seat, she fastened her seat belt, started the car and left in a cloud of dust.

They had finished fighting the fire and hit the main road more than ten miles south of the ranch. Zane had been the last one to turn onto the desolate stretch of road. There were no houses, no habitation for miles.

Ten minutes and seven miles later, Ellie saw a lone figure walking along the left side of the road. She slowed, downshifted and came to a halt beside him. Fumbling with her seat belt, Ellie freed herself and jumped out of the car and into Zane's arms.

The Compromise

He was filthy with soot, smoke and dirt, but she had never seen anyone look better. She clung tightly, tears falling.

"Shh, it's all right, Ellie," Zane said, putting his arms around her.

"I was so scared ... so worried when I saw that you weren't home this morning. Then Mike said you'd started home at seven, and it's almost nine now." She stepped back and wiped her eyes with her hands.

"I broke down and tried to radio for help, but the radio didn't work down in the valley, so I tried to fix the truck. I gave up a while ago and started walking. I hoped someone would come along," Zane said. Then he smiled at her. "I'm sure glad you came."

Ellie smiled back, still wiping away tears. "I'm sorry I'm such a baby. I never cry. I was so worried, though."

"Do you feel up to driving home, or do you want me to?"

"Would you?"

Zane nodded and waited for her to climb into the passenger seat and close the door before he got in, apologizing as he did so. "I'm filthy."

"Your back isn't, and besides, I don't care."

Zane turned the car around – a precarious feat on a narrow road with steep ditches on both sides – then started home at a more careful pace than Ellie had driven earlier. Neither spoke. It was enough for her to know that he was safe beside her.

Jo Maseberg

When Zane pulled into the yard and parked the car in front of Ellie's house, she said, "I'm glad you're safe."

Zane sat quietly for a minute, then reached for her hand and squeezed it gently. "I'm glad you came looking for me."

As they got out of the car, Zane handed the keys to her.

"What are you going to do about the firetruck?" she asked.

"It's off the road, so I'll get the part I need and go fix it, after I've had some sleep."

"Come get me," she said, walking slowly up the steps before turning to face him once more. "I'd like to come along."

"I will." Zane said, standing at the end of the walk. He looked at her closely and smiled. "I like your outfit."

Puzzled, Ellie, looked down, unsure whether she should laugh or cry and decided to laugh. She still wore her pajamas, the top a short-sleeve knit shirt with a bunny in the middle, the bottom a pair of shorts also covered with rabbits.

She shrugged, turned and went inside, shaking her head. Deep down, she knew that nothing else mattered. Zane was safe.

Walking slowly up to his own house, Zane wondered about his encounter with Ellie. He hadn't expected her to fly through the air and hug him, nor had he expected her to cry.

The Compromise

There's a lot going on behind those green eyes, he thought, as he opened the door to his house and stepped inside.

Ellie had been truly worried. Was she worried as a friend? Or was she worried because she saw him as something more? He hoped it was the latter, because what he felt for her was definitely something more.

That night, after fixing the firetruck, Ellie and Zane cooked supper together. Afterward, they collapsed in Ellie's living room, where several fans cooled the air. As Ellie worked on her units and lesson plans, Zane sat on the floor and flipped through textbooks.

"Look at this. A whole chapter on cowboys! Where were these books when I was in grade school?" he asked.

"I have no idea," Ellie said absently.

Sensing her detachment, Zane said, "And what about these stories in the reading books? They're actually interesting! And the teacher!" Zane's voice softened. "Look at those big, green eyes and that red hair."

Ellie glanced up, not quite sure that she'd heard right.

Zane grinned at her. "My teachers were never as interesting to look at. They all had gray hair and thick glasses ... and stern expressions."

Ellie laughed. "I can't imagine anyone being stern around you for long."

"I was quite the troublemaker ... still am. Ellie, thanks for coming to find me today."

"That wasn't trouble at all," she said. "I'm the one who blew everything out of proportion."

"I'll make you a deal," Zane said, drawing near. "You keep looking for me, and I'll keep being thankful, and no more will be said about it. Agreed?"

Taking the hand he offered and shaking it, Ellie nodded. "Agreed."

Chapter 15

Zane knocked lightly on Ellie's screen door and entered at her call. She sat on the piano bench, hands extended, fingers roaming fluidly over the keys, as a sonata poured from the instrument. The lamps from the living room reflected on the windows, and Ellie, too, projected an image onto one of the glass panes. For a moment, Zane watched the reflection rather than the woman.

Looking at the tilt of her head, the smooth curve of her back and the delicate lines of her arms, he knew that he wanted the chance to look at her for the rest of his life. How did she feel? How would she respond?

During the past two weeks, he'd been doing a lot of thinking, and today he had finally come to a conclusion. He loved her. He'd known that long ago, but now he knew what he wanted to do about it. His plan, though simple, would be effective, and he had few doubts. Tonight, he intended to initiate something he'd never tried before: courtship.

As the sonata ended, Ellie turned on the piano bench

and smiled. "What brings you by?"

Zane took a moment to smile back, then said, "Would you care to join me for a walk?"

"I'd like that. Just let me put some shoes on."

Minutes later, they walked out of the house into the darkness.

"Where are we going?"

"Down the pasture road, I guess. I don't really have a specific place in mind. Do you?"

"The pasture road is fine."

The night was dark and moonless, but Zane knew the ruts of the road and the turns in it without a light. It was hot, too hot, as it had been all summer, and now it was early August. At the end of the month, Ellie and the community's children would be returning to school, and he would not see her for most of the day.

"Feels like a storm," Ellie said softly, and Zane looked up at the sky. Cloud cover obscured the usually brilliant stars, and in the distance, flashes of lightning could be seen reflecting off the underside of the clouds. He could hear a far-off rumble.

"Sure does. I bet we'll get a lot of lightning, chance of fire and a phone call at three a.m."

Ellie laughed. "And aren't you the optimistic one!"

"I'm sorry, Ellie. Guess I'm just tired of no rain, tired of the heat and tired of being scared."

Now where had that last part come from, he wondered.

"Scared?" Ellie asked.

Zane examined his thoughts, and found that it all made perfect sense for once. "Yes. I've been scared for a long time that maybe, even together, we might not make this work. If we have to fail, I want to fail quickly and get it over with. I don't want to drag it out, thinking we'll make it and then fall flat. Do you understand?"

"Yes, I do." Ellie took a deep, shuddering breath and unconsciously reached for Zane's hand, for the support she knew she would find. "Dad and Mom felt the same way. That's why we sold when we did. But I've always wondered if maybe we had just fought a little harder and a little longer we could have made it work."

"Maybe your dad saved you a long, painful fight with a bitter end."

"The end was bitter enough," Ellie said.

Zane squeezed her hand, and for the first time, she realized that he held it. "I've noticed that about you, Ellie. You never say quit. If there's a problem, you hang on until you solve it, or it goes away. That's a good trait, but ... sometimes I think we've got to look more at what is really important."

"What do you mean?"

"Are your parents happy now?" Zane asked.

Ellie was silent for a moment, then replied, "Yes, I think they are."

"And they just pick up and go somewhere when one

The Compromise

of their children needs help, or when they want to get away, don't they?"

"Yes."

"Did they ever do that when they ran the ranch?"

A long silence followed, and Zane guided her steps as she became lost in thought.

Finally, she answered. "We never left the ranch for long periods of time, and we went only in the summer. If we were gone more than two or three days, we had to get someone else to come check the cattle. We could never leave in the winter during feeding."

"Did your parents make the right choice?"

"I can't say they did, and I can't say they didn't. They made the choice, and it's over now."

"Is it? Is it really over, Ellie?"

They had passed from the ranch yard through the open gate into the pasture and were walking up a gentle slope. The rumble of thunder was louder, but the lightning had stayed high up in the clouds.

At the first crack of cloud-to-ground lightning, Zane grabbed Ellie's hand and pulled her to a stop, then they both turned back toward the ranch. By the time they reached the yard, the lightning was striking loudly and repeatedly. They were running toward the house, their way illuminated by the flashes, when Ellie noticed something different.

"Rain!" she yelled at Zane in pure delight. "It's going to rain!"

Zane pushed the door of his house open a moment before the first big drop hit the dry ground, splattered upward and landed again. A moment later, the air was full of big drops of water falling to the parched earth.

They stood inside the door and watched the light show and the rain. After a while, the lightning moved on, but the rain stayed. The drumming of it on the roof sounded loud and unnatural to their ears, but it was the most beautiful sound in the world. Finally, Zane turned away from the door.

"How about a snack to celebrate?" he asked, heading for the kitchen.

"Sure, and a glass of tea or water would be good, too," Ellie said, gazing at the rain for another minute before following him. Zane dug a box of ice cream out of the freezer and set it on the table, then began to scoop it into bowls. Ellie poured them each a drink, and they sat down to eat.

"I can't believe it waited until August to rain," Zane said, scraping the last of his ice cream from the bowl.

Ellie rose and placed her empty bowl in the sink, running water into it as she gazed at the rain dripping off the eaves. "It knew Jill was coming. Maybe it likes her better than it does us, and it wanted to rain for her visit."

"Jill's here?"

"They got in this afternoon. She called and told me I had to make time to see her."

The Compromise

"Not the least bit pushy, is she?"

Ellie laughed merrily and found that it was easier to laugh now than it had been earlier. "It's August now, and while the clouds may think it's spring, I've got to get ready to go back to school. I need to get to town and buy some supplies and some more school clothes, and I need my hair cut."

"Sounds like you know exactly what you want."

Ellie didn't have time to respond. A noise from the other room sent Zane flying in that direction. Following at a slower pace, Ellie saw that he had been right to be worried.

"The roof is leaking!" she said.

"Yeah," Zane replied, mopping up puddles with a bath towel and placing buckets beneath the steady drips. "And if mine is leaking, guess what your thirty-year-old roof is doing."

Without saying goodbye, Ellie ran for the door. "My piano!"

Jill's arrival, coupled with the inch of rain received during the night, brought life back to the ranch. Ellie eagerly led the way to her garden, pointing to the fence she'd helped fix, to the haystacks she'd built and to the improvements she'd made about the house. Jill, grinning widely, followed, unable to get a word in edgewise.

Later, seated at Ellie's kitchen table, drinking iced tea and munching on homemade chocolate-chip cookies – Zane's favorites – they did some catching up.

"I was teasing Brian the other night that since all my favorite people lived in the hills, we should move home and practice medicine in the middle of nowhere."

Ellie laughed. "How did he take that?"

"Oh, pretty well. He said if I wanted to practice frontier medicine, all I had to do was say so. He offered to put up a tent for my operating room next to the windmill in Mike's north pasture – so I wouldn't have to haul water so far."

"The girls would have a great time in our little school," Ellie said. "I've got big plans for this year."

"Bigger than just teaching?"

"Now what do you mean by that, doc?"

Jill shrugged. "Let's just say that your eyes start to glow and you smile like a princess whenever any reference to a certain gentleman comes up. From what I've seen of him, I wouldn't say that he was beyond your charms, either."

Ellie fell silent, her gaze directed at a point far beyond Jill's left shoulder.

"Is this not a good subject?" Jill asked gently.

Ellie's eyes shifted abruptly, meeting Jill's. "To be honest, I don't know. Something inside of me says he's the one, and something else says, yeah, and his ranch isn't half bad, either. That's what scares me."

The Compromise

"Call it a package deal, Ellie. Kind of like buying hot chocolate and getting the marshmallows free."

"Bad analogy, Jill."

"OK, so I was never very handy at English. My meaning is the same. He's a great guy, and you two appear to be doing well together. Give this thing free rein and see where you end up. Don't just throw it away because of some misplaced sense of right. If he's the one, you'll know. Believe me, you'll know."

"You honestly think that?" Ellie asked, making rings on the table with the bottom of her tea glass.

"Yes. If he's interested, and you're interested, get to know one another."

Ellie nodded. "I think what you're saying is easier said than done. It's a small community. After living in the city, it was hard to remember just how small. If I hurt him, or if he hurts me, there's nowhere to hide. I can't just jump ship and leave the school, and I can't stay and never see him again, either. If I encourage his interest, or heaven forbid, initiate something, I won't be able to take it back. Neither one of us will be able to just pretend that something didn't happen."

"Pray, Ellie. Pray about it."

Ellie grinned wryly. "What do you think I've been doing for the past month?"

That evening, after Jill left, Ellie remembered that she

hadn't checked the mailbox. Zane, no doubt, had gone down earlier and sorted out his, leaving hers for her to pick up. Walking down to the box in the cool darkness, she breathed deeply of air that no longer smelled like dust. She could almost taste grass and water, and she reveled in it.

Opening the mailbox, she removed magazines and letters, feeling about in the darkness to make sure that the box was completely empty. Satisfied, she turned and wandered slowly back up the road toward the lighted houses. The stars shone brilliantly.

"You're such an awesome God," she whispered, craning her neck to look upward, bowled over by the sheer magnitude of the height and breadth of the night sky. "Show me, Lord. Show me the right way to follow, and guide me. Help me to make the right decisions. May I be a good teacher, and ... may I someday get the chance to be a good mother. Thank you, Lord. Thank you."

She couldn't bring herself to say amen. Too much remained unspoken, too much unsaid. As she neared the house, she knew that what she wanted more than anything was to be sure about her life and happy with that sureness. She had known what she wanted two years ago. Now, she wasn't so certain.

Unwilling to go inside, she slowed her pace and took measured steps up the walk. Zane's voice startled her, but somehow she had known that he was there.

The Compromise

"Wish I knew what to do, Ellie." His voice, and not his words, carried a depth of emotion that surprised her.

She threw caution to the wind and asked, "About what?"

"You."

She remained silent, waiting – half hoping – to hear the words she longed to hear, yet half afraid.

"Well, there's only one thing to do about it," he said.

"Oh?"

"You said something last night about going to town. We could go Friday, if that works for you."

"We?"

"I'd kind of like to be there if I'm going to buy you dinner."

Ellie felt her heart jump. Calmly, she asked, "Are you asking me to dinner, Mr. Redding?"

"Only if you agree, Miss MacCready."

Think, Ellie, think, she told herself fiercely. There's no going back. There's nothing to be done if ... But when did she ever think before she acted?

"I would be delighted, Mr. Redding."

She thought she saw the gleam of his teeth in the darkness.

"Good night, Ellie." His hand found hers and squeezed it gently, then he was gone. She groped for the porch railing and sat down hard on the step, forgetting the mail she had been so eager to read.

Jo Maseberg

Long after her normal bedtime, she was still sitting on the front step in the darkness, gazing intently at the stars and praying her heart out. She would have been surprised to know that Zane was doing much the same thing.

Chapter 16

Friday morning dawned fresh and clear, the world still dripping after a steady rain the night before. Ellie awoke slowly, hearing the birds outside her window before anything else. A fresh, cool breeze was blowing through her partially opened window, and she huddled beneath the thin sheet, shivering. Before she knew it, there would be frost, then snow. For now, however, the promise of August remained. The sun would soon warm things up, and she would be hot again.

She took a deep breath, yawned and opened her eyes. She remembered why she had been so excited last night. Today was the day Zane had promised to take her to dinner! She dressed hastily and headed to the kitchen for breakfast, filled with joy.

As she finished her toast and juice, the phone rang. For one elated moment, she paused, hand over the receiver, both wanting to hear Zane's voice and not wanting to lose the joy of anticipation.

"Hello?"

"Ellie." From the second she heard Zane's voice, she

The Compromise

knew something was terribly wrong.

"What is it?"

"Ben Thomson's dead. He died last night in his sleep. They just took the body, but Anna stayed at the house. As luck would have it, Kip Marcus, their hired hand, and his family are on vacation in Texas. Would you be willing to ... just go see her? You know her better than I do."

"Yes ... yes, I'll go right away."

Ellie replaced the receiver with trembling hands. She clutched her stomach, as though to protect it from the blow that had just come – Ben, dead.

Ellie remembered the tall, spare man with the kindly eyes and the gentle smile. She had known him all her life. He had scooped her up to ride in front of him on his saddle when she was less than a year old. He taught her how to rope, how to watch for sickness in calves and how to feed a baby kitten with an eyedropper. Living a few miles south of Ben and Anna, Ellie had often ridden her horse to their place just to help Anna with her garden or Ben with his fencing. Never had a day gone by when she had not included the older, childless couple in her prayers. And now Ben was dead.

Sobs caught in her throat, and she sank down, letting tears flow freely as she mourned.

Half an hour later, Ellie slipped behind the wheel of her car and drove to Anna's. As she pulled into the familiar yard, she half expected Ben to come out from

Jo Maseberg

the shop, wiping his hands on a ragged scrap of fabric, smiling in welcome.

She went to the back door and knocked. Moments later, Anna opened it. Wordlessly, Ellie opened her arms. As the older woman's eyes filled with tears, Ellie held her in a comforting hug. Anna's tears wet Ellie's shoulder, but Ellie didn't mind.

"I'm such an old fool," Anna said, stepping back and wiping her eyes with her hands in a childlike gesture. In a homemade, calico Western shirt, blue jeans, and a pair of scuffed and dirty boots, Anna looked like the ranch woman she had always been. Only her gray hair, cropped short now, and her lined face revealed her age.

"You're not old, and you've never been a fool," Ellie said. "May I come in?"

"Yes, yes."

Anna seemed to realize for the first time that they were standing on the back porch with the door open. "The cats will be comin' in soon if I don't get them fed."

Six cats with coats of yellow and white, black, and gray were mewing loudly on the step. Ellie smiled to see them. She followed Anna inside and let the screen door swing shut behind her. Anna reached into a corner where a sack leaned against the wall and scooped out a cupful of sweet smelling powder.

"Milk replacer," Anna said as she dumped the powder into a bowl. She added water and beat the mixture with a whisk until the milk was smooth and frothy.

The Compromise

"Can't remember when I started spoiling those cats this way. Seems like in the old days, I only gave them table scraps and expected them to catch mice."

Anna added a couple of handfuls of dry cat food to the bowl and paused, leaning against the battered old sink, lost in memory.

"Guess it was after calving five or six years ago," she said finally. "Had some milk replacer left over that the calves didn't need, and I didn't want it to go to waste. I knew I couldn't keep it up – stuff costs money, after all, but the cats liked it. Then, when that sack was empty, I came out the next morning and there was another one in its place. Ben never said a word – he always teased me about those cats – but every time I needed another sack, one was there."

Anna stopped talking as tears came to her eyes again. She reached with unsteady hands to lift the bowl, but Ellie stopped her.

"Let me – just this once."

Anna nodded mutely and held the screen door open. The cats jumped in eagerness and scurried around Ellie's legs as she carried the bowl to the feeding dish at the corner of the yard. As Ellie poured the mixture into the dish, the cats thrust their heads in, getting milk and food all over their heads and ears.

"Silly cats," Ellie said to them. "Now you'll all need a good after-breakfast wash."

Anna was leaning against the side of the house, tears

streaming silently down her face, when Ellie returned with the empty bowl.

"When I woke up this morning, he just lay there, so peaceful. I knew what had happened before I even checked for a heartbeat. They came and took him away a little bit ago. I thought I ought to go with 'em, but they said I could call with instructions or come into town later."

As Anna's disjointed sentences spilled out, Ellie nodded and listened quietly, reaching out once to touch the older woman's hand.

"We'll all miss him, Anna. He was a good man. The best."

Anna nodded, in control of herself once more. "Would you care for some coffee? I made some ... habit I guess, although I don't drink it."

"Coffee would be fine."

The ranch kitchen smelled of coffee and bacon. The counters, floor, table and sink were spotless, and the sunlight glinted off the shiny window panes. A fresh breeze blew in. It was cooler than it had been a month ago, the air ripe with the taste of fall.

Anna poured coffee into a mug and handed it to Ellie, then poured herself a glass of milk. Ellie took a seat. She realized, that more than anything, Anna needed someone to listen, someone to care.

"Winter's comin' on, and I don't know how I'm goin' to get through it without him," Anna said softly. "Kept

The Compromise

telling him that we should move to town and give up this crazy foolishness, but he'd just smile. Deep down, I know I didn't want to leave, either."

"Will you stay?"

Anna laughed without humor, raising dull, old eyes to meet Ellie's. "Stay? Even if Kip Marcus could feed two hundred cows by himself, I wouldn't let him. I may be old, but I'm not crazy. I wish that we could have had children. At least then ..."

"I know you don't have children, Anna, but I love you, and Zane and I will do what we can to help. Besides, doesn't Kip's wife work in town? I don't know if you can afford it, but they're good people, and I'll bet if you offered her a paycheck, Cheryl would be willing to help Kip feed instead of driving forty miles to work."

A spark returned to Anna's eyes, and she reached across the table to squeeze Ellie's hand. "Thank you, dear. It's so obvious, I guess I just didn't see it. It's just that, at my age, it's hard to lose your husband and then think of losin' your home at the same time. I was never one to wish for a little house in some little town. Ben, lyin' there this mornin', had a smile on his face. He went home to the Lord with a smile on his face because he died at home, listenin' to the crickets chirp. He died knowin' that the range got the rain it needed. He died knowin' that we'd make it through another year. He died happy, Ellie. When I go, who's to say that I'll have the same chance to smile?"

"If you sold out now, you wouldn't get anything for the cows anyway, the way the market is. The land would go easily enough, but who's to say you'll be better off in town with no family than you are here with neighbors who care? Give Kip and Cheryl a chance."

Anna closed her eyes and sighed deeply. "I'm tired all of a sudden. Would you ... would you get a piece of paper and a pen? I'd like to write down what Ben wanted done for his funeral, so that when they call, I can tell 'em."

Ellie nodded and moved to do Anna's bidding. She had a feeling that the day, already too long, would only get longer.

Four days later, Ellie and her mother stood beside Anna at the grave site. The small cemetery near an abandoned church felt lonesome with the tall, dead grass blowing in the wind, and yet, to a Sand Hiller, it felt like home. The wire fence nearby and the hill on which the cemetery was located gave a wonderful view of rolling hills.

The pallbearers stood across the grave from them, and Ellie studied them as she half-listened to the eulogy extolling Ben's virtues. Zane, dressed in black jeans, a white shirt and a string tie, stood with bowed head and folded hands. Beside him, dressed almost exactly the same, were Mike Snow and Frank Richards. Next came

The Compromise

Ellie's dad and her brother Mark, both in Western suits. Last came Ben's hired hand, Kip Marcus. Looking at Kip, Ellie easily could see where Christy's caring nature had originated. If anyone could get Anna and her ranch through the winter, it was this family.

"God help her," Ellie prayed. "Help her to keep her dream, and to go on without Ben."

A thought rose unbidden to her mind, and Ellie could not repress it. What would be better – to die and leave a spouse to grieve, or to die never having loved at all? With a thoughtful heart, she turned her mind back to the preacher's words.

When the simple service ended, Ellie let her mother and Cheryl Marcus look after Anna. She wanted – no, needed – a moment alone. Walking away, she drifted to the far side of the grounds, carefully avoiding old graves and headstones. As she let her mind drift, she breathed deeply of the wind and let it lift and stir her hair. Finally, she turned back.

Many neighbors had already left, but some remained. Zane waited near the pickup, talking with Mike and Peter. Closer still, Kip Marcus stood alone, obviously waiting to speak to her. She hurried her steps and reached him a moment later.

"Miss MacCready?"

"Yes, Mr. Marcus?"

"I need to speak with you. Do you have a minute?"

Ellie nodded and smiled a smile she did not really

feel. "I guessed as much. And please, call me Ellie."

"Then call me Kip."

They walked away from the open grave, back to the life of the hills. "Anna asked Cheryl and me to go partners in the ranch, with the provision that we get it all when she dies."

"That's good. She was talking about it, and I know it's for the best."

Kip twisted a baseball cap in his big hands. "Yes, but we'd been countin' on Cheryl driving Christy to high school. If she's to stay home and work with me, I don't want Christy to drive herself. She is so young. She just came out of eighth grade, and she's more than a little scared about that road. It would be different if there was another kid to drive with her, but there isn't. 'Sides that, the cost of the vehicle alone would break us. We could always board her out, but I don't think that would make any of us happy."

"I understand your problem, but what did you want to ask me?" Ellie asked gently, remembering her own high-school drive. She at least had had Jill to ride with.

"We're thinking of home schoolin' her."

Ellie thought about it for a moment. "That's a good choice. She's a smart girl and very self-motivated. She'll be a little lonely, but I think that would probably be best, at least until next year when Drew is ready to drive with her."

"That's what Cheryl and I think, too," Kip said,

The Compromise

relieved that Ellie agreed. "But we've neither one had much experience as teachers. Cheryl went to college, and I did pretty well in high school and in community college, but we're sure to hit a snag. We were wonderin' if you'd be willin' to help out – just once in a while," he qualified quickly. "We'd be willin' to pay you for your time."

"What do you want me to do?"

"Just help us find some good books and check on her once in a while. She really likes you, and I think she'd enjoy havin' you quiz her or push her a bit. You know what she's ready for, and we haven't got a clue."

"I'll be glad to help, Kip. I can give you some extra book order forms and help you decide what books to get. Christy won't need much guidance, but if she ever has any questions about anything, she can call me. In fact, why don't all of you come see me Sunday afternoon? We'll sit down and outline what you're going to do. You'll have to submit papers to the state, and I'm sure they'll ask for some kind of curriculum plan."

"Thank you," Kip said, taking her hand. "Thank you so much."

"I'm glad to help," Ellie said honestly. "Don't worry about paying me. You just get Anna through the winter. That will be payment enough."

As she returned to the pickup, and Kip joined his own family, Ellie realized that she had come here for a funeral, but now she was focusing on life again. *It's as*

Ben would have wanted it, she thought. "Get back in the saddle," he had always told her.

Zane held the pickup door open, then closed it carefully as Ellie seated herself, arranging her skirt before reaching for the seat belt. As he got in and started the pickup, she turned her head and looked at him thoughtfully. He felt her gaze and glanced at her. "What's that look for?"

"I was kind of wondering how I could ever have gotten through this without you," Ellie said. "But I was also wondering when you were going to keep your promise and take me out to dinner."

Zane grinned. "I guess tomorrow, if you're up for it."

"You'd better believe I'm up to it. School starts in a week, and after that, I won't get to town until Thanksgiving."

"Guess I'll be seeing a lot of you, then." From the expression on his face, Ellie surmised that he wasn't too put out by the idea.

"That's what I lo ... like about you. You're so easygoing."

Now why had she almost said love?

Chapter 17

Ellie's dinner date with Zane finally came to pass. There was no candlelight, and the meal wasn't all that expensive, but it was special. They had shopped all morning, first for ranch supplies then for school supplies and finally for groceries. Afterward, Zane drove to a steak house and parked the pickup in the nearly empty parking lot. They both ordered steak and baked potatoes, and for the next hour, they just talked. They shared childhood memories, worries about the present and hopes for the future. The drive home passed quickly as they continued their dinnertime conversation. When Ellie finally made it to bed that night, she knew without a doubt that she loved Zane for himself and not for his ranch.

School started a week later. Ellie walked swiftly down the gravel road early in the morning and inhaled deeply. The grass in the meadows was showing some promise, and Zane had decided to move the stacks off

The Compromise

of it. If the grass grew enough and if frost held off, they might get another cutting of hay.

"Please, God," she whispered. "We need that second cutting."

As she greeted her students warmly and handed out their books, she realized how much she had been looking forward to the start of the school year. Ellie had them start right in with their lessons. By midafternoon, she handed out lined paper and instructed them to write an essay for English.

"Instead of telling me all about what you did last summer, I want to hear all about the best time or the worst time you've ever had with your family. Just write it out as you think about it. We'll proofread and rewrite them tomorrow."

A thought came to her, and she held up her hand; the students looked at her questioningly. "No, on second thought, just write it like a journal entry. This is something only you and I will read and know about. You won't have to read it again if you don't want to. Just think back and put as many details into it as you can. This year is all about details."

"Why details, Miss Mac?" Drew asked, partially raising his hand.

Ellie looked from face to face. "Would anyone care to take a guess and answer his question?"

"I would!" Shayla Klein, now a fifth grader, offered.

"Go ahead, Shayla."

Jo Maseberg

"It's because details are important, right, Miss Mac?"

"That's right," Ellie confirmed. Confusion still reflected in many of her students' faces, so she elaborated. "Think of it this way. If I wrote a story about this summer, for example, I might say it was hot and dry and we didn't get much hay put up. Right?"

Everyone nodded in agreement.

"OK, that makes sense, because we were there – here, that is. We know it was hot and dry and the grass did not grow. Someone else, reading it without having been here, might think that was normal or wonder why it happened. What we need to put in is a detail – a very small one, but a crucial one. We need to tell people that it didn't rain."

Again, nods of agreement rippled through the class.

"OK then, the name of the game is detail. Get started. Sound out words, and if you really need help spelling, ask me."

Her eight students bent intently to their work. Ellie took a seat between her two first graders, Peter and Johnny, and helped them. Time flew, and it seemed as though only minutes had passed when the clock hit three-thirty. The students began to finish things up and put their books away.

Ellie stood and held up her hand for attention. "Is everyone finished with his or her essay?"

"Yes!"

"Uh huh."

The Compromise

"Real close."

Ellie nodded. "OK. If you aren't done, you have a minute to finish it. If that's not enough time, you may take it home and bring it back tomorrow. Everyone else, hand in your work."

Ten minutes later, the classroom was empty of students, and Ellie had every essay. She stood smiling, looking around the room at the clutter and the dust motes floating in the sunlight that flooded the western windows. At the far end of the meadow, she saw Zane with the tractor and hay sled, moving a stack. Suddenly, all she wanted to do was go home, put her feet up and read the essays.

She wiped the chalkboards clean, vacuumed the carpet and piled her books neatly on her desk in their original positions. Finally, she put her lunch pail and the essays in her backpack, turned out the lights, closed and locked the door, and walked home.

Later, seated comfortably in her glider with a tall glass of iced tea, she placed the essays on her lap and began to read, starting with the youngest student and working her way up to the oldest.

Peter's essay focused on the wedding of Jenny and Mike and on how much fun he had with his new cousins. Johnny Richards' essay told about going with his father to sell cattle. His older brother, Jimmy, now the lone third grader, wrote about how the whole family worked together in the hayfield. Ellie was still smiling at one of the hayfield anecdotes when she reached for Marcy Nichols' essay. The first line erased her smile. It read: *This is about the worst time in my life. This is about when my mom left.* The essay was heartbreaking in its simplicity, and Ellie wiped tears from her eyes as she finished.

She'd caught various references to not having a mother from the Nichols children before, but she had always assumed that their mother had died. Ellie placed the essay at the back of the pile and picked up the next one, noting that this one belonged to Kara Nichols, Marcy's fifth-grade sister. The first paragraph began:

The day my mom drove away was the worst day in my life. She just put her stuff in the car and drove off. It was winter, and there was snow. I remember the snow best and the frost. Frost stuck to the windows on the inside of the glass. I didn't think Mom would leave, but she did. She didn't even hug us goodbye. She just left, and the snow started to fall.

When Ellie had asked for details, Kara had taken her seriously, and reading Kara's essay brought tears and even sobs. When Ellie finally blew her nose and began to read the next essay, Shayla Klein's, she was relieved to find that it was another best-time essay, describing a family vacation to Denver. Alex Klein, her seventh grader, wrote not about vacation but about how wonderful it had been to hold his baby sister, Shayla, in his arms just after her birth.

Ellie didn't even want to read the last essay, but she

The Compromise

knew she had to. It belonged to Drew Nichols, her eighth-grade boy, the one who had, on the first day she met him, so proudly announced that he had two sisters. She dreaded reading another story of heartbreak. It began:

The day my mom left was the worst time my family ever had. I remember thinking that if I had been better, if I had helped out more, she might not be leaving. I had to hold Kara and Marcy while they cried because they wanted to go with her, and they couldn't. The worst of it was that she didn't even leave when my dad was home. Dad was out feeding the cows. She left him a letter then walked out the door. The air that came in when the door opened was so cold I couldn't breathe, and I thought, if I'm not good, and if I don't take care of the girls, Dad will leave too.

Finishing, Ellie placed the essays on the floor beside her chair and rocked silently, lost in thought. The depth of feeling and the seriousness with which her students had responded surprised her, and yet, it shouldn't have. She had a wonderful group of students, and she wanted to help them reach their dreams.

"Lord," she prayed, "grant me wisdom and help me to provide what each child needs. There are so many ways for me to reach them – for me to help them. Show me the best way. Amen."

That night, as Zane came in to supper tired and dirty,

Ellie met him with a smile and a hot meal. "Hey, stranger. How was your day?" she asked as he washed up in the kitchen sink.

"Got the stack-yard fence up and five stacks moved." Zane dried his hands and reached to gently tweak her nose. "How about you?"

"It was a good day," she said honestly. "A few tears, but a good day."

They sat down to a meal of hamburgers, potato salad and home-canned green beans. Zane blessed the food, and they began to eat.

"So, why the tears?" Zane asked, handing Ellie the salad.

"I had the kids write essays about the best or worst day they've ever had with their families, then I came home and read the Nichols children's essays."

Zane nodded, a look of understanding on his face. "The day Gracie left."

"Yup. I'm afraid I don't have a lot of kind feelings for the woman after what I read."

"There weren't many kind feelings for her, not before she left and not after it, either. Leavin' those kids like that was the worst thing she could have done. But I think we all knew she couldn't stay," Zane said.

"Couldn't? Or wouldn't?"

"Couldn't. She was a city girl with a degree in business. I don't know where she and Dale met, but they fell in love and married and came here. She did all right at

The Compromise

first and when the kids were babies, but when they got older, she started workin' at the bank in town. Then she wanted Dale to sell the ranch and move to a bigger town where there were more chances for the kids. Dale might as well have tried to rip his heart from his chest as sell out. The land is part of him and part of his kids," Zane explained.

"So she just left?"

Zane nodded. "I think she was goin' crazy out here. She couldn't handle the hills, or the wind, or the loneliness."

"But she left her children," Ellie said in disbelief.

"They're as much a part of this land as you and I are, Ellie. How could she take them away from the land they loved?" Zane asked gently.

Ellie met his gaze and smiled sadly. "It's hard, coming back to this community after so long. I know so much about so many people, and yet, I've missed out on a huge period of time. People I knew are gone, and new people have moved in. And some people have died."

"You fit in so well, I sometimes forget that you haven't been here forever."

"Thank you."

They smiled at one another, then turned their attention to more practical matters, discussing the grass in the meadow, the garden and the coming fall.

When Zane left at eight, Ellie leaned on the door frame and watched him go. Then she returned to the sink of dirty dishes. It did feel as though she'd been here forever, she thought. And it felt as though she would remain here for that length of time as well. She couldn't imagine going anywhere else, or living anywhere but here. She couldn't imagine not watching the children in her classroom as they finished growing and started lives of their own.

"You're in too deep, Ellie," she reminded herself as she finished putting away the dishes. But try telling that to her heart.

Jenny finished reading Peter his bedtime story and pulled the sheet up around him, kissing him on the forehead.

"Goodnight, Peter. Sleep tight."

"'Night, Mommy."

The first day of school had worn Peter out completely, she thought as she quietly left the room. He wasn't the only one. She was almost eight months pregnant and definitely starting to feel the strain. Just hanging laundry, baking bread and cooking supper had done her in. She moved slowly and carefully down the stairway and entered the study. Mike was hard at work on the ranch accounts, receipts and adding machine tape spread everywhere.

"Peter's asleep already," she told him, moving to stand behind him.

The Compromise

He looked up, concern in his gaze. "Are you all right, honey? Did you do too much today?"

"Yes, I'm fine, and no, I did not do too much. I'm just tired." Jenny rubbed his shoulder reassuringly. "You're the one who works too hard."

"I've been figuring out the money, and it looks like we can afford to hire someone to help out this winter."

"Once the baby is born ..." Jenny began.

"Once the baby is born, you will stay indoors and take care of him or her," Mike said firmly. "You can't take a newborn baby on the feeding tractor in the dead of winter. There's no need to harm you or the child just to feed cattle. We need a hired hand, and we'll get one."

"Who? How?"

"God will provide. Think of it this way: With all the free time you'll have, you can take up a hobby or two."

"You sure know how to make not being needed sound attractive," Jenny said, kissing his forehead.

"Sure I do. That's what I'm here for."

"Too bad everybody's not this lucky."

Mike grinned and turned the adding machine off before standing up. "Speaking of lucky, did you see Ellie today?"

"Just for a minute."

"So ... how is she?"

Jenny grinned. "Isn't this gossiping?"

Mike smiled innocently. "I thought this was a simple exchange of information between a husband and a wife, also known as communication."

They left the room, Mike turning off lights behind them, and headed up the stairs.

"In that case, I suppose I can tell you," Jenny said. "She said her dinner with Zane went well, and they talked a lot."

"Talked a lot?"

"Come now, didn't we used to talk?"

"Yes, but ..."

"I think we should just leave this whole thing in God's hands and worry about our own problems," Jenny said.

"What problems?"

"Well, I'd sure like to know whether we are going to be the parents of a girl or a boy, for starters."

Mike kissed her on the cheek. "For that, dear, you're going to have to wait about a month and a half. Until then, just keep guessing."

As Jenny crawled between the sheets to lay beside her husband, she hoped that Ellie would someday know the same joy, the same feeling of utter contentment. The baby kicked, and Jenny massaged the sore spot. She hoped that even though it was painful, that Ellie would one day know the wonder of having her own child. Life didn't end with marriage, after all. It extended into a future with years of day-to-day living, with the potential to become something truly beautiful.

Chapter 18

By mid-September, the grass in the meadow was tall and thick, waving in the warm breeze. Zane had finished moving the haystacks a week previously, leaving the meadow ready to be hayed once again. It felt strange, Ellie thought on her walk home from school, to be haying in September. The mornings and nights were growing cooler, heralding the coming of autumn, and blackbirds were gathered everywhere, their great flocks sprouting from the ground at a moment's notice to wheel, cawing raucously, as though they were a single entity.

The garden harbored pumpkins and squash that awaited harvest. Ellie had missed autumn in these hills. Tears sprang to her eyes at the sheer beauty that surrounded her. Since the rain, the sharp peaks and gentle swells of the hills were a soft green. The fan and tail on the windmill turned with a slight change in the wind. It groaned and began pumping clear, cold water into the cattle tank in the corral.

Ellie saw the pickup in front of the shop and knew

The Compromise

Zane waited for her. As she entered the house, she dropped her book bag by the door and hurried to change into jeans and a long-sleeved shirt. Tugging a cap over her curls, she stepped into the kitchen and grabbed a handful of chocolate chip cookies for a snack. Zane would have the water jug.

Closing the door, Ellie headed for the shop. As she approached, she saw Zane was using the grinder; sparks shot out in an arc of brilliance, made more so by the dim shop interior. She opened the door of the pickup, sat sideways on the passenger seat and worked her way through a second cookie, savoring every bite. A minute later, Zane turned off the grinder, doffed his helmet and joined her.

"Cookies?" he said in mock surprise.

"Want one?" Ellie asked, holding out her hand.

Zane swiped three of them and took a seat on an upturned bucket. They munched in companionable silence. Ellie finished first and jumped down from the pickup. She walked to the hydrant for a drink of water.

When Zane finished, he brushed his hands against his jeans and said, "Well, Miss Ellie, guess we'd best head to the field." He stood. "I got it all raked and swept after lunch and another good-size patch cut out this morning, so you'll have plenty to stack."

"That's good."

"How was school today?" Zane asked as he started the pickup and headed toward the hayfield.

Jo Maseberg

Ellie looked at him and smiled. "Crazy, but good."

"You're just a big kid at heart."

They arrived at the field a moment later, and Ellie saw that Zane had not been stretching the truth when he'd told her that he had it all raked and swept. There weren't more than two stacks worth, but it was ready. The loads of hay were divided roughly in half, the nearest bunch gathered around where the stacker was set up.

"Looks like things will move pretty fast," she said as the pickup rolled to a stop and Zane turned off the engine.

"Not too fast, but yes, faster than usual."

"I'll do my best to keep up," Ellie said, and she stepped out of the pickup and swung the door shut.

"You'd better," Zane warned as he got out, "or you won't get any supper."

He ducked just in time. A leather glove shot by his head, just missing him. The second glove didn't miss, though. Zane rubbed his arm where it had struck him and saw that Ellie was hightailing it to the stacker tractor.

"I'm just glad these are the Sand Hills and there aren't any rocks nearby!" Zane yelled after her. He laughed as he collected the gloves off the ground and placed them on the pickup seat. Five minutes later, he had the sweep started and headed out to bring in the first load. Approaching the stacker, he saw that Ellie had it start-

The Compromise

ed, and she was sitting on the iron perch waiting. It was hard to see her clearly, but he thought he detected a look of smug satisfaction on her face as he pushed the load onto the stacker head.

"Silly goose," Zane whispered. "Silly, wonderful goose." He had a plan, and Ellie didn't stand a chance.

The two stacks went up swiftly, and they finished by seven o'clock. Already, the sun was drifting toward the western horizon. Ellie waited for Zane to finish parking the sweep. She looked back at the tall, golden stacks and smiled. They would make it through the winter. They would not have to buy hay, would not have to sell the herd and would not have to leave the ranch.

"Thank you, God," she whispered, eyes closing in prayer. They had been blessed in so many ways.

Even as she reflected upon the bounty of the present, Ellie could not deny a niggling thought of the future. What would happen in the spring? Would she and Zane go on indefinitely as they were now? Or would they dissolve the partnership and go their separate ways? Or could they possibly ...

Zane's arrival interrupted Ellie's thoughts, and she climbed into the pickup, suddenly weary.

"I made some supper in the crock pot," Zane said as they neared the house, "if you'd care to join me."

Ellie nodded. "I'd love to."

Twenty minutes later, Zane prayed over Swiss steaks, baked potatoes and green beans. As they raised their heads, Ellie inhaled deeply and sighed in satisfaction. Zane just grinned.

"Lady, you look like you've never seen a decent meal."

"Let's just say that this is better than what I expected to have when you invited me over," Ellie said as she reached for a baked potato.

"Oh! Another insult like that and you won't be invited back, young lady."

"In that case, I humbly apologize. In fact, since you've been so good to invite me for dinner, the least I can do is return the favor and have you over for dessert and coffee."

Zane glanced at her suspiciously. "There's got to be a catch."

Smiling beatifically, Ellie sliced open the potato. "How are you at elementary math? I've got a lovely little pile of papers waiting at home, and I would certainly enjoy your company."

"You want me to grade papers?"

Ellie's green eyes sparkled as they met his, and she answered sweetly, "Well, they don't grade themselves."

By the second week of October, they had finished the second haying. They had almost doubled the number of haystacks in the stack yard. If the winter was fairly mild, it would be enough. If not – Zane didn't want to

The Compromise

contemplate the alternative.

Zane had something bigger on his mind, though: He loved Ellie, and he wanted to marry her.

When he checked the cattle Friday morning, he found his mind wandering. How could he make his proposal to Ellie special? He wanted to do something romantic. Money was tight, though. He could probably swing an evening out, but he couldn't afford a ring.

Ellie wasn't the kind of girl who would demand an engagement ring, but Zane wanted to do it right. As he finished checking the cattle and rode home, he decided that he needed help. He unsaddled his horse in the barn then turned him out to pasture. Back in the house, Zane washed his hands and reached for the phone.

His mother answered on the second ring; her voice comforting in its familiarity as she said, "Nurse's office."

"Yeah, Mom, it's Zane."

Genuine delight sounded in her voice as she asked, "What can I do for you, son?"

"I hate to call you at work, but I couldn't think of anyone else to ask."

"I'll do what I can, and don't worry about calling me at work. It's my lunch hour."

Zane took a deep breath and organized his thoughts before continuing. "OK, Mom, it's like this. I love Ellie, and I want to ask her to marry me ..."

"That's wonderful, Zane!"

"But I don't have a ring, and I don't see how I can afford one this year, and I don't want to ask her without one."

"That is a problem." His mother fell silent for a minute, then said, "Zane, I think I've got it."

"Yeah?"

"Great-Grandma's emerald ring."

"Great-Grandma's what?"

"Her emerald ring. It's nothing very big or fancy, but it's pretty and very delicate. I inherited it when Grandma died, and it has been sitting in the safe deposit box at the bank. Sheila never showed any interest in it, and it's really too fancy to just wear. I think it would suit Ellie perfectly, and I would be proud to have her wear it."

"Do you mean it, Mom?"

"You know I do. Now, when do you want it? I can get it out of the bank this afternoon."

Zane glanced at the clock. "Tell you what. I need to come get some things from Dad for the cattle anyway. Why don't I just drive up for supper and get it tonight?"

"That sounds great, son. I'll see you tonight."

"Thanks, Mom."

"I love you, Zane."

"I love you too, Mom. 'Bye."

Zane changed into good jeans and a Western shirt, then wrote a note to Ellie. He hung it on her door before gassing up the pickup and leaving. He arrived in

The Compromise

Valentine three hours later and spent the rest of the afternoon at the vet clinic with his father. At six, they headed home. As they pulled up to the house on the edge of town, Zane saw his mother's and Sheila's cars in the driveway.

"Been a while since both you and your sister were home," Marshal Redding said as they entered the front door.

"Daddy!" Sheila cried, rushing out of the kitchen, brown hair flying. Her normally serious demeanor had vanished, and Zane thought that her eyes were brighter and her cheeks more flushed than usual.

"Zane! When did you get here? Why are you here? Is Ellie here, too?"

Sheila hugged him tightly, not allowing him time for a reply. Zane returned the hug then pulled back and looked down into her hazel eyes.

"For your information, I came alone. I'm just here for supper and to pick up something, then I'm going home. How's college?"

"Good! I'm taking an overload this semester, and everything's wonderful. I'm taking a physics class, and it's better than anything I've ever done."

"You look happy," Zane said.

Sheila gave him an impenetrable look. "I'll tell you about it later," she said as their mother called them to the table.

Mystified, Zane headed for the bathroom off the

kitchen and washed his hands. His parents were already seated when he got to the dining room. Sheila placed one last steaming dish on the table and sat down. Zane took his place and bowed his head, as Marshal Redding said the blessing.

"Please pass the mashed potatoes," Sheila said, and Zane glanced at her again before helping himself and doing as she asked.

As the clatter of spoons in serving bowls gave way to peaceful dinner conversation, Zane couldn't help wishing that he and Ellie would someday have children to share the table.

"So, do you want to tell them why you're here?" Clara asked her son.

Zane hesitated for a moment. Then he realized that she had not told the rest of the family about their morning phone conversation.

"Well, I'm going to ask Ellie to marry me."

"Wonderful!" Sheila said, clapping her hands in excitement.

"Congratulations, son," his father said.

"I haven't asked yet," Zane reminded them.

"Then we'll be praying for you," his mother assured him. "I think you're perfect for one another."

"I hope so, Mom."

They finished the meal with the easy talk of a close family, then Zane's parents offered to do the dishes and let the siblings talk for a few minutes before Zane had to

The Compromise

leave. Sheila led the way outside, and they began to walk slowly down the block.

"I've been meaning to call and talk to you," she said, tearing a blade of grass with her fingers.

"I've called a couple of times, but your phone's always busy, so I just gave up," Zane said with a smile. "That's a pretty busy life you have at college."

Sheila turned her gaze to the sidewalk and kept it there.

Zane could see that something was bothering his sister. "OK, Sheila, what's goin' on?"

"You're not the only one looking at marriage," she said. "Ever since the Fourth of July and that week at the ranch, James MacCready and I have been calling each other. Lately, we talk for an hour every night, and sometimes longer. Yesterday he ... he proposed."

"And you said?" Zane prompted gently.

"I said yes." Sheila looked up, tears in her eyes. "I love him so much."

"And I take it you haven't told Mom and Dad?"

"I don't know how. James is ten years older than I am. What will they say?"

"You might be surprised. Besides, you've got to tell them someday. You don't want to marry him without Mom and Dad being there, do you?"

Sheila shook her head. "No."

"I'll back you up, if you want to tell them tonight."

"I don't know if I can."

"Sure you can."

"How?"

"Well, start by saying, 'Mom, Dad, James MacCready asked me to marry him, and I accepted,' ... or something to that effect."

Ten minutes later, they were all gathered in the living room. Sheila sat beside Zane on the couch and looked at her parents and their expectant faces.

"Mom, Dad, I have something to tell you. James MacCready asked me to marry him, and I said yes."

They were surprised, but they weren't angry.

Zane gave his sister's hand a squeeze then rose. "I think you all need to talk about this, and I need to get home."

He said his farewells and walked to his pickup, anxious to get home and see Ellie.

The dainty emerald ring was tucked safely inside his shirt pocket, with the flap buttoned over. He couldn't ask her tonight, but he could plan when and where he would ask her. He had plenty of time to think on the long drive home.

Chapter 19

Monday, when the alarm rang at six a.m., Ellie woke to find the wind howling and her bedroom frosty. Curled into a tight ball beneath her comforter, she wondered how cold it actually was.

The summer is finally over, she thought. And it had been a long summer. Usually the first frost came in September, but it was already the third week of October. Ellie could remember having snow by this time in past years.

As she lay huddled in bed deliberating the merits of getting up, the phone rang. With a groan, she sat up quickly, swung her bare feet to the floor and reached for the phone. She grabbed the covers and wrapped them around her before answering.

"Hello?" She could see her breath in the air.

"Morning." As she heard Zane's cheerful, familiar voice, she smiled.

"Good morning to you, too. Are you the person to blame for this weather? I heard you complaining about the heat yesterday."

The Compromise

"Nope, I'm afraid you can't pin it on me. Weather comes from a higher power."

"Sure. You didn't pray for it, either, I suppose."

"Anyway," Zane continued, ignoring her jibe, "I was wondering if you'd like me to come start your furnace and the stoves at the school, too."

Relief flooded through Ellie at the thought of warmth, and she nodded decisively, forgetting for an instant that he couldn't see her, before replying, "Yes! Please, come start it."

"I'll be over in fifteen minutes."

Ellie hung up and ran to get dressed. By the time Zane arrived, she was wearing blue jeans, a forest-green turtleneck with matching cardigan, and heavy hiking boots. A kettle of water was starting to steam on the stove. Zane wore his heavy work coat. In one hand he held a box of matches, and in the other, a pair of pliers.

Fifteen minutes later, musty-smelling hot air was blowing into the house from every vent, and the water was boiling.

"Take your coat off and stay awhile," Ellie said.

"I'll stay, but I don't think I'll take my coat off just yet."

Zane took a seat at the table and ducked as a dishtowel came flying through the air.

"Hey!"

Ellie just smiled and poured cocoa mix and hot water into two cups. She handed one to Zane then took a seat, placing her cup on the table. "It's sure starting to feel like winter."

"Aren't you glad we got the haying done when we did?"

"Yep." Ellie took a sip of cocoa and let it trickle down her throat.

Zane, watching, smiled at her look of happiness and chuckled softly. "You look like a cat who just lapped up a bowl of warm milk."

Ellie's eyes met his, and she said, quite seriously, "I don't know whether to be flattered by that or not."

"I'll tell you what, Miss Ellie, I love that look."

Ellie glanced down at her cocoa, unable to continue meeting his gaze, unable to convince herself that what she saw shining from those gray eyes was love.

"It's almost seven," she said a moment later. "Will you come to school and light the stoves?"

"I will do better than that. I'll drive you there and start the stoves, but only on one condition."

"What's that?"

"How about a slice of that pie you made yesterday?"

Ellie smiled and rose to get plates and forks. "You've got yourself a deal."

By eight-thirty, the propane heaters were blowing hot air into the schoolroom, and Ellie's students were settling down to work. Outside, the wind howled down

The Compromise

from the north. Just after lunch, the low-hanging clouds began to spit tiny, white flakes. For half an hour, the students and Ellie stared out the windows, mesmerized by the first snow of the season. The snow melted on contact with the ground, but that didn't matter: For thirty minutes, it had snowed.

After school, Ellie gathered up her lunch pail and book bag, dreading the long walk home. She had finished most of the grading during the day, so her bag was fairly light. She knew that the bitter wind would cut right through her jeans and hat, even though her coat was warm.

Locking the door to the schoolhouse, she rounded the corner of the building and saw a pickup sitting outside the barbed-wire fence in the tiny parking area. Had one of the parents waited to speak with her? A moment later, she saw that it wasn't a parent at all; it was Zane. She brushed her mitten-covered hand across her eyes and rubbed away tears that weren't solely brought on by the wind.

"Hi, stranger," Zane said as she opened the pickup door and crawled in. The heater was on, and the cab was warm. Ellie turned to thank him, searching for the words to tell him how she felt, when Zane reached unexpectedly across the cab and brushed two gentle fingers across her cheek. As he drew his hand away, she saw drops of moisture on it – tears.

"It's cold out there," Zane said softly, before stepping

on the clutch and putting the truck in reverse. They started slowly down the gravel road, and Ellie couldn't think of a thing to say.

When they arrived home a few minutes later, Zane parked the pickup between their houses, and they both got out. Zane grabbed Ellie's book bag and carried it to her door, handing it to Ellie as she entered. She set the bag and her lunch pail down, then turned and saw Zane standing on the step. Without knowing why, she stepped forward and hugged him tightly, tears springing to her eyes once more.

Zane's arms encircled her, and for a minute, she stood still, her cheek pressed against his coat, which smelled of hay and the shop. How could the simple act of coming to get her from school have affected her so deeply? All those days when they had worked together, side by side, and she had known that she had loved him, she had managed to keep from touching him, to keep from letting him know her feelings. Now, after a tiny act of kindness, she had fallen apart.

Maybe it had something to do with the fact that his being there had felt so perfect, so right. When she crawled into the cab, she had felt as though they were married, had been married for years, and it was the most natural thing in the world for him to come get her, to touch her, perhaps to even offer a kiss and ask her how her day was. I love him, she thought. I love this man more than I've ever dreamed I could love anyone.

The Compromise

And he's holding me back. Is he being a friend right now, or is there something more?

She finally looked up, and saw that, just inches away, he was looking down. He had such a tender, caring look in his eyes that she knew instantly, without a doubt, that it was very likely he loved her in return. The gap between them seemed to close, and she knew he was going to kiss her. Wanting it and fearing it at the same time, she leaned closer, then the telephone rang.

The shrill ring startled them both. Ellie remained where she was a second longer, then suddenly Zane's arms fell away, and she ran to answer the phone.

"Hello?"

"Ellie? It's Mike. Jenny's gonna have the baby. Could you come get Peter and his stuff and look after him until we get back? We're going to leave now. He'll be OK until you get here, but we've got to go – now."

"Slow down, Mike," Ellie said, hearing pure panic in his usually calm voice. "Yes, I'll come get Peter. Are you going to make it to the hospital in time?"

"I hope so. Oh, Jenny wants to talk. Honey, you can't. We don't have ..."

Mike's sentence trailed off as Jenny grabbed the phone.

"Ellie, don't listen to a word he says. We've got plenty of time. This baby may come faster than Peter did, but things are starting nice and slow. I think we'll make it clear to Ogallala. Despite that, Mike still has to gas up the pickup – yes, dear, you do need to – so take your time. We'll probably still be here when you get here."

Ellie hung up and turned to face Zane, who had stepped inside and shut the door behind him.

"What is it?" he asked.

"Jenny's having the baby, and I need to go get Peter. He'll stay with me until they get home."

"I thought he was going to stay with Laurie."

"So did I, but I think Laurie took her boys to town this afternoon to get groceries before winter sets in for good. She's probably not back yet."

"Then we'd better go get him now," Zane said.

As they headed for the pickup, Ellie couldn't help but feel cheated. The tender moment was gone forever, and she wondered if they would ever reach that point again.

"Ellie?" Zane said as they started up the gravel road past the schoolhouse, headed for the main road.

She glanced at him expectantly.

"You won't get away so easily next time."

Ellie turned her head to look out the side window and found that she was unable to restrain her grin.

Ten minutes later, Ellie and Zane watched as Mike and Jenny drove out of the yard, Jenny waving and Mike clutching the steering wheel. They watched until the pickup was out of sight, then they walked slowly toward the house where Peter was getting his clothes

The Compromise

and things together for an overnight stay.

"I've never seen Mike so nervous," Ellie said. "I hope he gets them there in one piece."

"It's his first child," Zane said. "If I were in his shoes, I'd be nervous too."

"Whatever for? It's the woman who does all the work," Ellie teased.

"It's hard to step back and let someone else do something that difficult. I think it would be harder still to watch someone you love experience such pain."

"All right, I can see that," Ellie admitted. "Pain or no pain, I want a lot of children someday."

"Oh you do, do you?"

"Yep. At least five," she said seriously.

"Why not six? Then you could have three boys and three girls."

"That's a thought."

What kind of thought, she did not elaborate. They reached the house and walked in to help Peter finish packing.

Later that night, Ellie ladled steaming chili into bowls and she, Zane and Peter sat down to supper. Afterward, Zane and Peter played a game while Ellie finished grading schoolwork. When the phone rang, Ellie answered it. Ten minutes later, she returned to the kitchen and told Peter and Zane the good news.

"Peter, you're a big brother!"
"Wow! Is the baby a boy or a girl?"
"A girl."
"Great! I wanted it to be a girl," Peter said, grinning.
"Why?" Zane asked him.
"Because," Peter explained, "when I'm out with Dad all the time, Mom gets lonely in the house by herself, and as I get older and older, she'll need some company."
"Girls can go outside and help, too," Ellie reminded him gently.
"Sure, and I can show her what to do and help her."
Ellie wondered if Peter had another reason for being pleased that the new baby was a sister rather than a brother. A brother, in Peter's reasoning, might take his place with Mike, whereas a sister was an entirely different matter. She knew, though, that as time went on, Peter would learn that Mike loved him as a son no matter what and that no one could ever take Peter's place.
"Hey, Ellie," Zane said, interrupting her reverie.
"Yes?"
"I laid your mail on the table by the door when I came in. You got a couple of letters today."
"Thank you, Mr. Postman," Ellie said, leaving the room to retrieve the forgotten mail. She saw that she had a letter from her parents and one from her brother James. Ellie opened the one from James first. So shocked was she by his news that she read the letter three times.

The Compromise

James, her brother James, was getting married. At the age of thirty, it was about time. Still, he was marrying Sheila, Zane's sister. In a year, or less than that, she would be related to Zane.

She didn't want to be related to him. She wanted to be married to him.

As the thought crossed her mind, she looked up guiltily, wondering if Zane had somehow sensed it. He was moving his game piece back five spaces, much to Peter's delight. For a moment, she wondered what kind of father Zane would make. A good one, she decided. He would love his children, would treat them with the same consideration and kindness with which he treated her.

"Oh, Ellie?" Zane asked, looking up.

"Yes?"

"Did they say what they named the baby?"

"Rose, after Jenny's grandmother."

"That's a pretty name."

"I helped decide," Peter said proudly, his soft, brown eyes glowing.

"You're a very lucky boy, Peter," Ellie said. "And you'll be a good big brother."

Peter smiled beatifically. "I know. I know."

Chapter 20

The air was crisp, and the warmth of the sun felt good on Ellie's back. She was on her hands and knees in the potato rows, waiting for Zane to dig holes. When the dirt came up, she reached in and took potatoes out of the holes.

"Oh, this one has arms!"

Ellie held an especially large potato aloft.

He laughed with her. As she tossed the potatoes into the wheelbarrow next to them, Zane shoveled through the dirt once more, shaking out two small potatoes she had missed. Zane stepped backward, and Ellie moved forward, toward the end of the row.

"We have three hills to go!"

"You counted, huh?" Zane asked absentmindedly, sending the shovel deep into the earth. Ellie shifted her position, then cried out as a large sandbur became embedded in her knee.

"Are you all right?"

He let go of the shovel and dropped to the ground beside her as she reached to remove the sticker.

The Compromise

"Here, let me."

With work-roughened fingers, Zane took careful hold of the bur and pulled it out, tossing it back into the rows they had already harvested.

"Thank you," Ellie said softly, wiping a tear from the corner of her eye. "That hurt worse than the cactus the other day."

"Are you OK?"

"Yeah, I am now."

"Then let's finish this."

They moved quickly, and when the last of the potatoes were in the wheelbarrow, Ellie stood, marveling at what they had accomplished in two afternoons. Zane wheeled the last bunch to the pickup and dumped the potatoes into the back where the rest of the day's harvest lay. They would not go hungry this year, not with the fruits of their labor in the cellar.

"Let's get these spread out to dry before putting them in the cellar," Zane said.

Ellie walked stiff-legged across the potato patch and sat on the tailgate of the pickup. Zane started the engine and drove slowly toward Ellie's house. A large tarp was spread on the lawn and they spread the potatoes out to dry in the sun.

Tomorrow, they would begin weaning the calves. Weaning meant that feeding would begin. Winter was coming, and time was flying. Still, Ellie could not deny that she was longing for a time of cold winter nights and warm evenings by the fire. Winter brought a certain peace and a certain yearning. She wrapped her arms around herself as a sudden chill swept across the back of her neck. She could yearn all she liked, but she might as well face the facts: She would probably be as alone when winter ended as she was now.

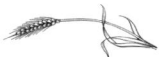

"Yip, yip, yip! Come on, get up there, old girls!" Ellie yelled, wheeling her horse around to bring in two cows that were straggling behind the main herd. Husky calves bawled and started as the herd moved steadily toward the corrals. Their sleek, black mothers answered them in kind, adding to the din.

On opposite sides of the herd, Mike and Zane moved their horses back and forth, keeping the cows together and moving. Sitting easily in her own saddle, Ellie kept the back of the herd together. Far ahead, at the very front of the herd, Zane's sister, Sheila, drove the feeding tractor, pulling the hay sled. Luring the cattle onward worked better than forcing them to go. Still, they had spent a long morning on horseback, rounding up the herd.

Thirty minutes later, Ellie herded the last of the stragglers into the corral, and Zane, now on foot, swung the gate shut. The roiling, teeming, bawling herd kicked up dust and dirt in the corral, and Ellie knew that now the real work was about to begin. She dismounted and tied

The Compromise

her horse next to Zane's and Mike's.

Walking to the fence where the others were gathered, Ellie asked, "Where's the tractor?"

"I parked it on the other side of the corral, behind the windbreak," Sheila said.

Dressed in blue jeans and a Western shirt, with her hair in a ponytail, Sheila looked the part of a cowgirl. But her sneakers gave her away as a city girl.

"Well, Zane, what's the plan now?" Mike asked.

"We'll sort the calves from the cows, and turn the cows into the west pasture and meadow. Then we'll vaccinate and feed the calves."

"When will your dad get here with the vaccine?" Ellie asked.

"About the time we'll need him, if he left when he said he would," Zane said, glancing at his watch. "Let's get started."

Zane and Ellie herded a small bunch of cows and calves into the alley, and Mike and Sheila worked the gates. Sheila opened one gate to let the calves into a large pen to the left, while Mike opened a second to release the cows into a pen to the right. Sheila and Mike kept a running count of the cows and calves, and when they had finished, they gave Zane the totals.

To Zane's relief, every animal was accounted for, but they did another count to doublecheck. Afterward, they got on the horses again and moved the cows to the west pasture. By the time they had finished and got back to the barn, Ellie saw that Marshal Redding had arrived.

"Why don't we have lunch before we start with the calves," Ellie said. "I'm hungry."

"What'd you cook for us, Zane?" Sheila asked, with a laughing glint in her eyes.

"Yeah, Zane, what?" Mike echoed.

"You'd better just come and find out for yourselves."

The kitchen was warm and filled with the scent of pot roast, potatoes, carrots and onions. Ellie set the table, and Zane emptied the contents of the crockpot onto a platter. He sliced the roast while the others washed up. After lunch, Sheila and Ellie cleared the table, and the men headed back to the corral to get set up.

"Is it OK if I stay overnight tonight, and maybe part of tomorrow before heading back to school?" Sheila asked as Ellie filled the sink with hot water and soap.

Ellie glanced at her, smiling. "I'm really not the one you should ask."

"Well, I really just wanted to talk to you. Zane won't care. In fact, he would have liked for me to come and stay last night rather than having me drive in this morning."

Ellie put glasses into the water. "I'll bet you had a really early morning."

"Oh, I was up at four a.m., but I'm an early riser anyway, and I got about eight hours of sleep last night. What I really wanted to do, though, was spend the evening with you."

The Compromise

"Any special reason?" Ellie asked as she began to wash the glasses.

Sheila leaned back against the sink and looked at Ellie, saying quietly, "I don't have a lot of really good friends. When I marry James and end up in Colorado, I have a feeling that I'm going to be lonely, and well, I'd like to get to know you better. I think we could be friends, and I'd like to have someone I could just call and talk to, for no reason at all, and I ... I guess I'd like that someone to be you."

Ellie stopped washing dishes, and she turned to face the tall, slender young woman. "I'd like that, too."

Sheila's answering smile was so bright and cheerful that Ellie understood instantly how easily her brother had fallen in love with her.

The rest of the afternoon went by swiftly. The calves, after receiving their shots, were turned into the big corral where Zane had moved in two rows of feed bunks. Later, they drove the tractor and hay sled back into the corral and dumped piles of hay for the calves to eat.

Weaning was always a traumatic time for the calves, Ellie knew. Suddenly cut off from their mothers, the calves would bawl day and night for about a week. During the summer, they had learned to graze the pastures, but now they would have to learn how to eat cottonseed cake and hay.

The week of weaning would be stressful for Zane and Ellie as well. The slightest thing – headlights after dark, loud noises, even coyote songs – could frighten the nervous calves. At any given moment, they might suddenly stampede and lunge into the corral fence, either taking it down or getting hung up in it. No matter what the result, calves would be hurt.

Zane and Ellie's situation was different than Mike and Jenny's. Next Friday, Mike and Jenny would round up their herd, cull the calves and send all the steers and the smaller, less desirable heifers to the sale barn. They would wean only the replacement heifers. Zane and Ellie had weaned the whole calf crop and would feed them until January. Then they would cull the herd and sell all but the best replacement heifers.

That night, Ellie could hear the plaintive cries of the calves. She knew the cows in the west pasture could hear the sounds, too, and were, no doubt, lined up against the fence, bellowing their pain beneath the sliver of moon.

"And I'd be bellowing, too," Ellie said aloud.

"What?" Sheila asked from her position on the floor.

"Just talking to myself," Ellie said as she turned back from the window and let the curtain fall into place. "Weaning is a tough time on both the calves and the mommas."

The Compromise

"Downright heartless, if you ask me," Sheila said. "Still, it has to be done. Everybody has to grow up sometime, even calves."

"You're such a fountain of wisdom."

Sheila's eyes twinkled merrily. "That's what James says, too."

"You love him."

"Yes."

"And you've only seen him ...?"

"Four times, total. He came to the college to see me three times, and the fourth time was here, when we met. But I feel as though I know him better than I know myself. Some nights, we talk for hours on the phone. That's what I love best – our talks."

"When are you thinking of having the wedding?"

"Next summer, definitely. I'd like to see him more before I actually just up and marry him."

"How are you going to manage that?" Ellie asked, taking a seat in the glider.

"He's accepted a five-month position at an office down the street from the college, so we'll be living in the same town all spring."

"That's nice."

Sheila sighed. "Well, I hope so. It's kind of scary having him make that kind of career decision just to be near me. What if it's the wrong thing to do? What if I'm the cause of it?"

"Breathe, Sheila," Ellie said with a smile. "At least

you and James know what you want and are going for it. Something special happened, and now you've found your life's mate."

"Your turn will come, Ellie."

Ellie smiled sadly. "I'm not so sure. Still, I have much to be thankful for."

Later that night, after popcorn and a movie, Sheila headed back to Zane's house. The yard light was on, illuminating the corral, and the bawling of the calves filled the night. Upon entering Zane's house, she followed the light into the living room where Zane was sitting, almost asleep in his chair.

"Hey, brother," she greeted, flopping down on the couch.

"Hey, yourself. How's Ellie?"

Sheila shrugged. "Let's just say that you're not making your intentions very plain to her."

"What's that supposed to mean?"

"Well, if you think you're just going to ask her to marry you, and she's expecting it and going to jump for joy, you've got another thing coming. From what I heard tonight, she has no clue that you love her and no hint that you're going to marry her. She's resigned herself to being an old maid."

"Nice try, Sheila. You almost had me going for a minute there."

The Compromise

"I'm not kidding, Zane. I wouldn't – not about something this big."

"Then what should I be doing, oh wise, engaged one?"

Sheila looked exasperatedly at him. "Oh, I don't know. Maybe kiss her, hug her or tell her that you love her. Pick one, she's a woman."

"Actually, I've got a plan."

"Oh, you do?"

Zane nodded. "I made reservations for dinner next Saturday night. We're all going to be in town to watch Mike and Jenny's calves sell and to get groceries. I plan to surprise her."

"Oh, she'll be surprised."

"You've got quite a case against me tonight. What's up?"

"Listen, the only time I ever went to the sale barn, I just about fainted from the dust, the smoke, the stench and the noise. After she endures a day of that and, oh yes, buys a month's worth of groceries, you're going to take her out to supper – in cowboy boots and jeans, no doubt – and propose? It'll be a miracle if she doesn't faint at the table."

Zane massaged his aching forehead, then closed his eyes.

"What works for you, Sheila, might not work for Ellie. She's a ranch girl, born and bred. She loves the sale barn, and she's been looking forward to Saturday

Jo Maseberg

in town for a month now. She'd be more shocked if I took her out in a tux to a five-star restaurant, which, by the way, Ogallala doesn't have."

"OK, big brother, have it your way."

Zane looked steadily at her for a moment, then they both began to laugh.

"I'll bet you've got James wrapped around your little finger," he said, finally.

"Oh, not completely, but it won't be long now."

Zane shook his head as he got up. "Good night, little sister."

"Good night, Zane."

As he was leaving the room, Sheila called out, "And Zane! Good luck; you'll make her a good husband."

Soon, he promised himself. Very soon.

Chapter 21

Ellie's week began on a good note but grew progressively worse. She didn't know if her students were affected by the coming of Halloween, or if the stress of weaning the calves was taking a toll on them. But within the span of a week, each one had developed a behavioral problem that left Ellie feeling frustrated and tired. The girls suddenly didn't like the boys; the boys didn't like the girls either. Her three youngest boys forgot how to read, and her oldest boy complained that he didn't have enough reading. Each recess brought a scrape or fall and a bout of tears.

By Friday afternoon, Ellie had had enough. She dropped her grading on the kitchen table, grabbed a snack and headed toward the summer range for a walk.

The hills were in full fall array. Blackbirds warbled cheerfully, and as she left the ranch yard behind, Ellie noticed a rabbit hiding in the grass, watching her, its nose twitching. Her hiking boots dug deep into the sand as she started up a hill as she left the road and took to the hills.

The Compromise

"Lord," she prayed as she walked, "Thank You for getting me through this week. I just don't know how I would have managed if it hadn't been for You. Be with each family this weekend and help the children get their rest so that we may start with a clean slate on Monday. Help me rest too."

Getting rest would be difficult, she knew. She had promised to go to town with Zane, Mike, Jenny, Peter and baby Rose. They would spend all day Saturday at the sale barn, and Ellie knew that she wouldn't be home until late Saturday night. Sunday there was church, and after that, she needed to grade papers. It was a never-ending cycle.

She'd been looking forward to this Saturday for almost a month, but suddenly she felt too tired even to get in the car and ride to town. She knew she had to go; it would be fun. She loved sale day, loved the sale barn and everything that went with it, and it would be wonderful to go shopping, even if it was only for essential items.

By the time she got back to the house, she felt a little better, although she was still tired. She had been looking forward to her Friday night ritual with Zane – pizza and a movie – but a note on her door said otherwise. He was helping Mike move the cows in closer, and Jenny would feed him supper. He didn't know when he'd be back. It also said that they wouldn't need her help in the morning. They had enough help without her.

"In other words, I don't count for much," Ellie muttered aloud, grimly reading the note once more.

She hadn't seen Zane for more than an hour during the past week, and that hour had consisted of a few minutes snatched here and there in passing.

Well, I can take care of myself. I'm a big girl, Ellie thought to herself as she crumpled up the note and dropped it in the kitchen trash before grabbing her car keys and heading out the back door. She checked the oil in her car, added gas from the ranch tank and washed the windshield. Then she parked the car near the road; it was ready for the early morning drive to the sale barn. She had volunteered to take Jenny and the baby. Peter would be riding with Mike in the pickup, following the cattle trucks. Zane, she assumed, would be taking his own pickup to town after feeding the calves.

Ellie heated a plate of leftovers in the microwave, watched an old movie and went to bed. When her alarm beeped at six a.m., she reluctantly crawled out of bed and headed for the shower. It woke her up, and by the time she returned to her room to hunt through the closet for the day's apparel, she felt cohcrent enough to make a decision. She chose plain blue jeans, a soft, creamy, short-sleeved shirt and a dark-green, Nordic-print sweater.

For breakfast, she grabbed a cinnamon roll and a glass of juice. Then, taking a pile of grading, she sat down and began marking papers. Just after eight a.m.,

The Compromise

she put her things aside, grabbed her keys and purse and went out the door.

By the time she reached Mike and Jenny's place, the car was warm inside. Driving past the corrals, she saw that the trucks were gone and the cows had been turned out. The replacement heifers remained, a small group pressed tight against the gate leading to the pasture. She parked next to Zane's pickup, but saw no sign of him.

"About par for the course," she muttered to herself.

Jenny opened the door and came out before Ellie had gotten halfway up the walk.

"I'll buckle the car seat in the back, if you'll hold the baby," Jenny said.

Ellie smiled in return. "That I can do, and gladly." She took the baby carrier and diaper bag. Pulling back an edge of the blanket, she saw that the dark-haired baby was asleep, her tiny, sweet face wrinkled just a bit, as though in the middle of a dream. Minutes later, Jenny had the car seat fastened securely, and she buckled the carrier into it.

"That is really neat," Ellie said as she watched the process.

"One of the latest things," Jenny replied, checking one last time that all the straps and fasteners were secure before taking the diaper bag from Ellie and putting it on the floor. Then, very carefully, she closed the car door. "Makes it so much easier."

Both women got in and buckled up. As they left, Ellie

glanced toward the corrals, but saw no sign of Zane.

"I'll sure be glad if they sell fairly early today," Jenny said, leaning back into the comfortable seat.

"Any special reason?"

"Mike and I are going vehicle shopping."

"Really?" Ellie was surprised. Thinking it over, however, she realized that it made sense. "The pickup only holds three, doesn't it?"

"Yes, and my car died three weeks ago. We haven't gone anywhere as a family since the baby was born. I know times are tight, but I've got a savings account that I inherited from Grandpa, and there's enough in it to pay for something new to drive, especially if we trade in the pickup."

"Anything particular in mind?"

Jenny smiled. "We've talked about it. We know the gas mileage will be awful, but we want a double-seated pickup. With the roads like they are, we want something with four-wheel drive, so we can get out in the winter if we have to."

"That's wise," Ellie said. "So you'll be riding home in a new pickup tonight, and I'll be all by my lonesome."

"You can ride home with us, too," Jenny said. "Or better yet, you could take the kids, and Mike and I could ride home alone."

"Oh, no you don't! I love children, and especially yours, but after the week I've had ... let's just say I'm glad Rose isn't old enough to talk yet."

The Compromise

"That bad?" Jenny asked, laughing.

"That bad."

It was almost ten o'clock by the time they reached the sale barn. The gravel parking lot was nearly full, and cattle trucks were lined up from the corrals to the highway. Ellie parked in the middle of the lot and helped Jenny get the baby and her things out of the car. Together, they walked to the front door of the sale barn. A rancher held the glass door open for them, and they shivered as they stepped into the lobby.

The lobby bustled with buyers, sellers and family groups. Ellie saw Drew, Kara and Marcy Nichols with their father, checking in at the sellers window. They waved at her, and she waved back.

"Should we grab a book or two, or just go on up?" Jenny asked.

"Tell you what, I'll grab a book, and you start up."

Ellie got two books listing the lots of calves and their owners. She met Jenny at the stairway going up to the arena.

"Do you want me to go ahead and clear the way?" Ellie asked.

"Sure."

When they reached the top, they stood still a moment, searching the crowd for Mike and Peter.

"There they are, about halfway down on the right," Ellie said, pointing.

"OK."

With a chorus of "excuse me," "oops" and "sorry," Jenny and Ellie wove their way through the crowd to the seats Mike had been saving for them. At the same time, a bunch of teeming, surging red-and-white calves exited the ring and another group came in. The auctioneer's litany continued without pause, until finally, just as Ellie reached an empty seat, the room resounded with the cry, "Sold to buyer one-eighty-five. Mark 'em down for eighty-seven."

Glancing back down the row, Ellie saw that Mike had taken charge of Rose. He had her in his arms, the blankets almost completely hiding her. The baby was so very tiny, so very young. Looking around the three-sided arena, Ellie saw other fathers with their babies. The noise, dust and cold air didn't seem to be bothering anyone, and she remembered that as a child, she had loved to come here. She still did. It felt like coming home.

Mike's calves hadn't sold yet, and Ellie checked the book to see where they were listed, not that the order of listing would give any idea of when they would sell. About an hour later, as Ellie marked down another ranch's cattle sold, Jenny leaned over and nudged her.

"Mike is going to go look at the calves in the pens and see how long we might have to wait. Do you want to stretch your legs and go with him?"

The Compromise

"That sounds good."

Ellie rose and followed Mike back up the steps to the exit doors then down the steep steps once more to the lobby. They passed through quickly, with Mike returning a few greetings as they went.

When they got outside, it was cold, but Ellie's sweater was warm, and the air felt good on her cheeks.

"To the corrals?" Ellie asked. Glancing up at Mike, she saw that in his gray felt cowboy hat, denim coat, black jeans and black boots, he looked like one of the "good guys" from one of Zane's Western movies.

"Yes, ma'am."

He sounded like one too, Ellie thought with a smile as she walked beside him. They mounted the steps to the walkway that overhung the corrals, and Ellie stepped back to let Mike lead the way. They walked past pen after pen of calves. Closer to the barn, Ellie saw the pen riders – men on horseback – moving groups of cattle up the long alleys to the arena. Other riders were bringing groups out and putting them in shipping pens, where they would be loaded onto cattle trucks and hauled away.

"Here we are," Mike said suddenly, and Ellie saw that they were above a series of pens holding Black Angus calves.

"These yours, or are you just claiming them for the day?" Ellie teased.

"Oh, I reckon they're mine. Tomorrow I'll let some-

Jo Maseberg

body else claim them." Mike glanced down the alley. "Looks like we've got plenty of time before they'll sell. We can go get some lunch. After lunch, you and Jenny probably can get some shopping done, too."

"Be nice if they'd sell around four or five this afternoon, wouldn't it?" Ellie said.

"Yeah, it would be."

Mike turned, and they started back, squeezing against one side of the walkway so that a group of men could pass them. When they were once more walking abreast, Mike reached over and squeezed Ellie's shoulder.

"How are you holding up?"

"Me?" Ellie was surprised. "I'm doing all right. In fact, it's almost like I never left. So many things remain unchanged. The electronic scale is new, and the computers, but in many ways, it's as though time stood still."

"Just think. You'll be back in January with Zane's calves."

Ellie nodded. "Yes, I guess I will be."

And they would be Zane's calves. They weren't hers, and no matter how well she felt she fit in again, she really didn't. She had a tenuous hold on this life, and when spring came and times got better, that hold would be broken too.

It would be time to go back to the real world, and stop pretending that she was here to stay. For the first time,

The Compromise

she allowed herself to face the truth, and it hurt. The sense of melancholy that came over her threatened to bring tears, but she refused to cry in front of Mike.

They ate lunch in the sale barn restaurant, filling a booth with their little group. When they were about halfway through, Zane joined them. After lunch and another check of the pens, Ellie and Jenny went shopping.

They drove through car lots, and Jenny looked at the big pickups. They narrowed the search down to one lot that Jenny and Mike would visit later. After purchasing everything but the groceries, Jenny and Ellie returned to the sale barn.

At four p.m., Ellie was settled in between Mike and Zane, and Mike's calves were brought into the ring.

"Ladies and gentlemen, we've got some good black cattle here from Mike Snow's operation. Mike, would you care to stand up and show us where you are?" The auctioneer's voice resounded through the room as he looked over at Mike.

Mike stood up with Rose in his arms. Jenny and Peter stood beside him.

"Who's that new little face I see there?"

"This is Rose, and she's just about two weeks old,"

Jo Maseberg

Mike said proudly.

The auctioneer grinned widely and winked at Mike. "Tell you what – you keep the calves, and I'll take home the little lady."

Everyone chuckled, then the auctioneer returned to the business at hand.

Mike and Jenny's calves did better than most other lots by about three cents a pound, but the prices weren't near what Ellie had seen in the past. Still, it would be enough to get them through the year.

The drought, Ellie reasoned, had probably caused more ranchers to sell more of their herds than they normally would have, and that drove prices down. She held out hope that selling in January would be different, that Zane would get better prices. He needed a good price – there was no doubt about that.

Mike leaned over and said, "We're going to wait about an hour for the check, then go buy that new pickup, get the groceries and have supper. You two are welcome to join us, or go your own way. I know it's been a long day for everybody, but Jenny and I want to thank you both for your help."

"You're welcome," Ellie said.

Zane grinned. "You owe me, Mike. You'll be on horseback come January. That's thanks enough."

Yes, it would be Mike on horseback in January, just like it was Zane on horseback this morning. I'm not needed, Ellie thought. Not really. They just humor me.

The Compromise

She was a schoolteacher, plain and simple, and it was best if she accepted that and went on with life.

Zane looked at her. "You want to go get groceries now, Ellie? Then we can get some supper and head home."

At least I'm good enough to go grocery shopping with, she thought.

"Sure," she said, smiling wanly. "That'll be fine."

Chapter 22

"Thank you," Ellie said to the grocery boy as he wheeled the carts back to the store. The groceries were safely tucked away in the cab of the pickup and Ellie's car. The grocery store was their last stop before going to dinner.

"I'll meet you at the restaurant," Zane said as he opened the pickup door.

"All right."

Ellie slid into the car and started the engine, waiting for Zane to lead the way. As the car heater blasted cold air, she shivered.

They would be heading home soon. She had grading to do, and she wanted nothing more than to sit down with a cup of hot cocoa and a warm blanket.

Dinner with Zane would be fun, though. She had barely talked to him all week. Even today, while sitting together in the sale barn, they had barely spoken. They were too busy watching the cattle and listening to the auctioneer.

They drove across town to the restaurant and parked

The Compromise

next to each other. Ellie grabbed her purse, locked the car and pocketed the keys. She waited for Zane to lock the pickup.

"Ready?" she asked.

"Yes."

He grinned at her, a rather feeble grin, she thought.

"You look really pretty today."

Ellie was surprised, and she knew her face showed it.

"Thanks. You're not too bad yourself."

He could be a heartbreaker, she thought, in that striped Western shirt and those blue jeans. He needed a haircut, but she liked the way his brown hair curled up at the collar of his shirt.

They reached the door, and Zane held it open, ushering her inside.

"Table for two?" the busy hostess asked as they waited to be seated.

"Reservation for Redding," Zane said.

Ellie looked at him in surprise then followed the hostess as she wound her way through the room.

Zane seated her at a quiet corner table for two and took his own seat. The hostess placed menus in front of them and disappeared. Ellie looked at Zane and saw that he still seemed a little uneasy.

She smiled reassuringly and opened her menu, saying as she did so, "You should have warned me that I needed to dress up. I didn't realize we were going somewhere so ..."

Jo Maseberg

"Fancy?" Zane suggested, taking his cue from her and teasing in return.

From the harness hung on the wall to the fish tank in the corner, the restaurant was a far cry from fancy. The other diners wore jeans, boots and Western shirts; most had been at the sale barn. The waitresses wore denim skirts, and the tablecloths were red-checked.

"So, what are you hungry for tonight? Fried, baked or grilled?" Ellie asked as she perused the menu.

"Steak and a baked potato sounds good to me."

"And it comes with bread," Ellie said.

The waitress returned and they both ordered steak and iced tea. When she left with the order, they looked at one another earnestly. Then, as if by some unwritten accord, they began to discuss the sale, the prices and the people they had met. When the steaks arrived, they ate slowly, savoring the time together as much as the meal.

When the waitress cleared away their plates and brought coffee, Ellie leaned back in her chair and let her eyes close briefly. The turmoil of the last week drained from her as she listened to Zane talk. Then the conversation shifted, and Ellie opened her eyes.

"Ellie, I–I know we haven't seen much of each other this week, and I'm sorry. Things have just been so crazy."

"That's all right. I think it was a busy week for both of us," Ellie said.

Zane took a deep breath, and his steady, gray eyes

The Compromise

looked into her green ones. "I missed you, Ellie. I missed you more than I've ever missed anybody in my life, and you live right next door. Anyway, what I wanted to tell you tonight was ... well, I love you, Ellie."

Ellie looked at him in shock, not sure she had heard him correctly. As she looked, he turned his eyes away, reaching into his coat pocket for something. An instant later, he handed her a small, velvet-covered box.

She took it, confused by his sudden declaration of love. She opened it, and a beautiful emerald ring glittered in a bed of black velvet.

"Ellie, would you be my wife?"

Ellie stared from the ring to Zane, and a torrent of emotions flooded through her. She had hoped that he would grow to love her. She had wanted it more than anything. But after the past week, it seemed so improbable that she could not believe it.

"How can you love me? You ... you've never even kissed me. You act more like a friend or a brother most of the time. Besides that, lately, you don't even seem to want my help on the ranch. I can't face this right now, Zane, I really can't. I'm sorry."

Ellie stood up, tossed her napkin on the table and blindly fled the restaurant.

When she reached the parking lot, the cold air drove the last vestiges of warmth from her body. She fumbled in her purse for the car keys and finally got the door open. She dropped into her seat, fastening her seat belt a second before starting the engine. Flipping on the lights in the gathering dusk, she shifted the car into reverse and backed out of the parking space. Then she changed gears, hitting the main road out of town less than a minute later.

Zane stared in shock at the empty seat and the open box beside the half-drunk cup of coffee. The waitress came around the corner, bearing the coffeepot in one hand. She took a look at the empty chair and the table. Then she looked at Zane, a softness coming to her weary face.

"I'm so sorry, mister."

Zane managed a nod. "Could you ... could you bring me the check?"

"Sure."

A moment later, he tucked the ring back into his coat pocket, paid the bill and headed toward the pickup. Ellie's car was gone, he noted with a sense of foreboding. She must have gone home. How was he going to face her again? He had been so sure ... so sure that she loved him, so sure that she would return his love. His sister had been right after all. He started the pickup and slowly drove home, feeling more tired than he'd ever felt.

The Compromise

Ellie drove as if the devil himself was chasing her. The road was mostly empty. As she passed a slow-moving pickup, she tried to understand what Zane had been thinking. She accelerated and flew past a large, green-and-white striped, double-seated pickup, her mind racing faster than the car.

Mike drove slowly, conscious of the precious load he carried – Peter and Rose slept in the back seat. A small, red car moved up fast behind him and passed on a downhill stretch of empty road, and he looked after it.

"Isn't that Ellie's car?" Jenny asked.

"Looks like it," he said quietly.

Jenny reached for his hand. "If it was, she's driving awfully fast."

"About eighty, I'd guess."

"Could something be wrong?" Jenny's voice reflected concern.

"Zane was going to propose to her tonight."

They rode the rest of the way home in silence, lost in thought and prayer. They wanted the best for Zane and Ellie, but they had no control over the situation.

When Zane arrived home, he saw Ellie's car parked near the back door of her house. He drove by and parked near his own house. He took his time unloading the groceries, then put them carefully away. It looked to be a long, lonely evening, and nothing could release the invisible band that had tightened around his chest.

After the frantic drive home and the haphazard

unloading and unpacking of the groceries, Ellie collapsed on the floor in the middle of the living room and cried. When her tears were spent, she bowed her head and spent the next two hours thinking and praying. As peace came to her soul, she knew what she had to do.

She rose, washed her face and drank a glass of water before screwing up her courage and walking out the door.

It was nearly ten o'clock when Zane heard something that sounded like a knock. It was repeated a moment later, and he rose and hurried to answer the door. He opened it and saw Ellie standing on the porch. He stepped aside and motioned for her to come in. She did, and he closed the door. She wrapped her arms around herself then looked up at him, her back ramrod straight, shoulders back.

"I want to alter our compromise," she said expressionlessly.

She was leaving, then. She wouldn't stay, and it was all his fault.

He finally managed to ask, "What do you want changed?"

"The land title. I want my name on it."

"But ... I thought ..."

She looked at him, her green eyes brimming with tears once again. "You can leave your name on it. Just

The Compromise

insert 'Ellie' right after your first name, before your last one."

"Do you ... do you mean what I think you do?"

Ellie nodded, and saw that his eyes bore unshed tears as well. "If the offer still stands, I'd be proud to be your wife."

Zane didn't wait for her to change her mind. He pulled her close, and for the first time, they kissed. Wrapped in his arms, Ellie knew that she had made the right decision. She would never regret it, never wish to take it back. She was willing to give up everything in the world except this man.

"Want some cocoa?" Zane asked, brushing her hair back from her forehead.

"I'd love some."

They moved into the kitchen, and Zane put a pot of water on the stove. Ellie took a seat on one of the worn kitchen chairs and watched him put cocoa mix into two mugs.

"I hate to bring it up, but why the sudden change of heart?" Zane asked, dropping spoons into the mugs and turning to look at her.

"Surprise, mostly." Ellie sighed softly. "Actually, to be honest, I spent all day telling myself that I didn't belong here, that I should leave in the spring, that you were nothing more than a good friend. I just about had myself convinced, when you upset the apple cart, so to speak.

"You completely surprised me. I didn't expect a thing, then you offered me a beautiful ring and the chance to be your wife, and I ... I just ran away."

"Speaking of rings, would you like yours now?"

Ellie nodded, the lump in her throat too big to swallow.

Zane disappeared into the other room and returned with the box. He opened it, took the ring in his fingers and reached for her left hand. She offered it, watching as he slid it on her finger.

"Perfect fit," she whispered, eyeing the delicate, beautiful stone.

"Kind of like you," Zane said softly. "You're a perfect fit in my life."

"That, sir, just earned you another kiss."

The whistling of the teakettle interrupted them, and Ellie watched as he fixed the cocoa. He set a brimming cup of hot, rich chocolate with marshmallows in front of her then took a seat across the table.

"We've got a lot of decisions to make," he said, meeting her gaze.

"Such as?"

"Such as how soon do you want your name on that land title."

Ellie smiled, shaking her head. "We have time, don't we?"

The Compromise

Zane shrugged. "I was just thinking that last week when we were only friends, I saw you less than ten minutes a day. This week, we're engaged, and I'll be lucky to see you ten minutes all week."

Ellie laughed with him and nodded. "I suppose it wouldn't hurt to consider things tonight. I know I'm too wound up to sleep."

"All right, then. When do you want to have the wedding? I know Sheila's planning on getting married sometime next summer, but they don't know when."

Ellie remained quiet for a few minutes, thinking. "I know this may sound like I'm rushing things, but how about by Christmas?"

"Any special reason why?"

"Oh, a few." Ellie's eyes twinkled, but her tone remained serious. "I think that, despite our failure to communicate, we're meant to be together, and we don't need to wait. Besides that, with money as tight as it is, it would be best to start sharing living expenses sooner rather than later."

"And you're afraid I'll back out on you," Zane teased.

"Yes, that too."

"Next question: Big wedding or small?"

"Small," Ellie answered firmly. "We can't afford anything big, and I'm not that kind of girl. I'd rather have something small, with just family members and close friends."

"When?"

"Do you have a calendar?"

Zane reached up and took down the one on the wall. They bent over it. "OK, how about after the school Christmas program?"

"That would be great. My family could come for the wedding, then stay and look after things while we went on a honeymoon. Then we could come back and have Christmas with everybody," Ellie said.

"Or, we could get married on Christmas Day, let our families hold down the fort and come back after Christmas. That way, if your brothers wanted to come, they wouldn't have to miss the wedding or take extra time off because of work schedules."

"It might be less stressful to have it Christmas Day," Ellie agreed. "Besides, Christmas is my favorite day of the year."

"It's set then."

"It is."

Ellie looked at Zane then yawned widely, one hand moving to cover her mouth.

"I think it's my bedtime after all."

"I think so too."

As he hugged her good night, she couldn't help but wonder what she had been thinking earlier. This was where she belonged. In less than two months, she would be Mrs. Zane Redding.

"Thank You, Lord," she whispered as she walked home beneath the bright stars.

Chapter 23

Halloween came, and with it the end of weaning. The calves were turned out into a pasture near the house, where Zane fed them every morning and night. Plans for the wedding progressed rapidly. They mainly consisted of long distance phone calls to invite their families and their friend Mike's sister, Jill. The pastor agreed to perform the service, and they secured the church for Christmas night.

On Thanksgiving, Ellie and Zane left the ranch in the hands of Mike and his new hired man and headed south to Kansas. Ellie hadn't realized how much she missed her family until she walked in the door and her mother welcomed her with a hug. Zane, too, was welcomed with open arms. The day after Thanksgiving, Ellie and her mother drove to Dodge City to shop. Ellie picked a pattern for her wedding dress, and they bought material, thread and trim. The next day, they drove back to Nebraska.

School seemed to fly by, as Ellie and her students prepared for the annual Christmas program. Along with

The Compromise

two plays that Ellie had written with Zane's help, the students were learning group songs and solos. Ellie felt as if half the day was spent with her fingers on the piano keys, but she wasn't complaining. In fact, she loved every minute of it.

The parents got involved when Ellie sent home notes asking them to find things to use as costumes and stage props. By the second week of December, with the program just a week away, Ellie was ready to make the trip to the old community hall with the props, students and costumes.

Zane went down early that morning and started the furnace, then Jenny and Ellie drove the students down just after school started. They left everything in the vehicles except for the cleaning supplies. Without removing their coats, they went to work in the chilly, old room. They swept up spider webs and debris from the past year, dusted the old church pews that lined the walls, and washed the windows. It was lunchtime before they finished. Seated on the now clean pews, the students ate their cold lunches and chattered excitedly while Jenny and Ellie sat back and watched.

"I hope Mike's feeding the baby," Jenny said as she reached for her sandwich.

"He's probably spent all day inside with her. He dotes on her so much," Ellie said.

"That's true."

"How are we ever going to be ready to put this pro-

Jo Maseberg

gram on next Wednesday? We can only come back one more time to practice," Ellie said.

"You'll be ready. You always are."

In the end, Jenny was right. By Wednesday night, the old building had been transformed. The room was warm, which was good. A sudden cold snap had lowered the outdoor temperature to ten below zero, and the hooks lining the walls by the back door were full of coats, hats and wraps. The community had turned out in full, though. The women brought cookies, candy, cider, cocoa and coffee. The students circulated through the crowd, handing out hand-made programs.

At seven p.m., the students disappeared backstage, and Ellie stood before the old, painted canvas curtain, waiting for the crowd to become quiet.

"Ladies and gentlemen," Ellie said, "we welcome you to the Sweet Valley Christmas Program."

Then, stepping aside, she moved to the electric piano set up in the corner, and volunteers raised the curtain. The students, dressed in their Christmas finery, took center stage, singing "Deck the Halls" with their own special gusto.

From then on, the evening passed in a blur. Ellie coached her younger students with their lines, played countless songs and never once stopped smiling. At the end, the students gathered once again and sang "We Wish You a Merry Christmas."

It brought down the house. The applause went on

The Compromise

and on, and finally, flushed and excited, the students bowed once more, then headed offstage to look for their families. Ellie was about to stand up and announce that snacks would be served at the back of the room when Mike surprised her and took center stage, holding a large, red-and-greed wrapped gift. The room turned silent, and Mike turned to Ellie, beckoning her to join him.

"Folks, just a year ago, a very special lady came and helped us out of a real bind. She stepped in to teach the kids when we couldn't find anyone else, and she did a good job. In fact, I'd say she's done an excellent job."

Mike waited for the applause to fade, then continued.

"She's not only been a good teacher, but a good neighbor as well, and since she's decided to marry Zane, she will continue as both. The school board and the parents would like to take this time to offer our congratulations and a gift to Miss Ellie MacCready."

Mike handed Ellie the package, then gestured for her to open it. She set it on the table in the center of the stage and did as he bid. She opened the plain box and discovered that it contained only tissue paper and one small envelope. To the laughter of the crowd, she opened the envelope and pulled out a card, which she read aloud.

"Dear Miss Mac, this is an invitation to your bridal shower, immediately following the annual Christmas program."

Jo Maseberg

Ellie's voice was lost as the entire room shouted, "Surprise!"

She could only cry as her students, their parents, and neighbors she barely knew came up and offered her gifts in all shapes and sizes. Someone, Jenny, she learned later, sat her down in a chair, pushed a table by her, and offered her a box of tissues. A minute later, with Zane at her side, Ellie began opening the gifts. The generosity and the spirit in which the gifts were given overwhelmed her more than once. Sometimes, all she could do was laugh. Along with dishes, towels, blankets and appliances, she received a rope to keep her new husband close to home, a small calf-pulling chain, for the same purpose, and her own kit of veterinary supplies.

After the initial uproar died down, everyone partook of cookies and hot drinks. Around ten p.m., the guests left, and Mike, Jenny, Laurie, Zane and Ellie cleaned up, loading the props into the back of Zane's pickup and the gifts into Ellie's car. In a giddy, exhausted state, they drove home, and Ellie realized, as she collapsed into her bed, that only a week remained until her wedding.

The day before Christmas Eve, Ellie's family and Zane's sister arrived. Robert, Ellie's older brother; his wife, Sarah; and their two children, Shane, five, and Karrie, three, had flown to Denver from California.

The Compromise

They rented a van and drove the rest of the way with Mark and Annie, who had also flown in. James had followed in his own vehicle. Ellie's parents drove in.

Ellie was even more surprised, though, when Jill and her family drove into the yard.

As Jill hugged Ellie tightly, she said, "We haven't even gone to Mike's yet, but I had to see you."

"It's so good to have you here," Ellie said, hugging her in return.

On Christmas Eve, Zane's parents drove in to celebrate with the clan. Zane's house felt as though it were bursting at the seams, but it was a wonderful, happy time. Ellie fell asleep that night with Sheila on one side and her niece Karrie on the other, unable to comprehend that, after all the planning and rushing, tomorrow was Christmas – and her wedding day.

On Christmas morning, the men fed the cows while the women cooked a huge feast for dinner. Ellie and her mother were closeted in Ellie's extra bedroom with the sewing machine. Her mother finished fitting Ellie's dress and hemming it.

"Have you seen Zane yet this morning?" Grace MacCready asked her daughter.

Ellie laughed softly. "He swiped a cinnamon roll off my plate at breakfast. I threw my spoon at him, and he disappeared."

"You're as bad as children," her mother teased, her needle darting in and out of the dress.

"We've had to be too serious too often. I think we've agreed to be lighthearted as much as we can."

"Are you ready for the wedding?"

"For the wedding? No. For the marriage? Yes."

"Good. I'm so pleased that all of my children have chosen such good partners."

"Thanks, Mom."

Three hours later, after the conclusion of the church service, the congregation was dismissed, but Ellie and Zane's families remained. Mike, Jenny, Brian, Jill and all the kids stayed as well. Zane waited at the front of the church in a neat black suit. The gentle strains of organ music filled the small sanctuary and at an unseen signal, changed to the wedding march.

Everyone turned to look as the back doors opened, and Ellie stood framed between them. A wreath of creamy roses and ribbons rested upon her red hair instead of a veil. Her dress, made of cream-colored satin, resembled a medieval lady's gown. The square neckline framed her mother's pearl necklace while the long sleeves flared and fell gently to her hands. The skirt fell straight down, just touching the ground.

Another measure of the music passed, and Ellie marched down the aisle on her father's arm, a look of serenity upon her face. When her father handed her to Zane, she kissed her father's cheek, then took Zane's

The Compromise

hand. As the words were read over them and they repeated their vows, Ellie knew that now, at last, the compromise was over. Now it was a promise that bound them – a promise of faithfulness, honor and, most of all, love. No matter how hard the times got, no matter how crazy, she would always have Zane, and he would always have her.

As he slipped the delicate gold band onto her finger, she looked down and said a brief prayer. "Lord, be with me and with this man who is now my husband. Guide us in Your ways, that we may do our best for You, each and every day."

As she sent a silent amen heavenward, the pastor said, "You may kiss the bride."

Ellie looked up into her husband's eyes and heard him whisper softly, "This is one promise I intend to keep."

She closed her eyes and sealed it with a kiss.

Jo Maseberg will graduate in May with a Master's degree in English from Kansas State University in Manhattan. Growing up on a ranch in the Midwest, Jo lived the life she writes about. She enjoys teaching English composition classes and, in her spare time, writes and spends as much time outdoors as possible.

Fireside Library

Other books by OGDEN PUBLICATIONS

These Lonesome Hills	Letha Boyer
Home in the Hills	Letha Boyer
Of These Contented Hills	Letha Boyer
The Talking Hills	Letha Boyer
Born Tall	Garnet Tien
The Turning Wheel	Garnet Tien
The Farm	LaNelle Dickinson Kearney
The Family	LaNelle Dickinson Kearney
Lizzy Ida's Luxury	Zoe Rexroad
Lizzy Ida's Tennessee Troubles	Zoe Rexroad
Lizzy Ida's Mail Order Grandma	Zoe Rexroad
Many to the Rescue	Zoe Rexroad
Carpenter's Cabin	Cleoral Lovell
Quest of the Shepherd's Son	Jaunita Killough Urbach
Martin's Nest	Ellie Watson McMasters
Third Time for Charm	Mabel Killian
To Marry a Stranger	Glenda McRae
Pledges in the West	Glenda McRae
Sod Schoolhouse	Courtner King and Bonnie Bess Worline
Texas Wildflower	Debra Hall
River Run to Texas	George Chaffee
Home on the Trail	Mona Exinger
Horseshoe Creek	C.P. Sargent
The Longing of the Day	Louise Lenahan Wallace
Dr. Julie's Apprentice	Don White
The Bargain	Jo Maseberg
The Ghost of Whitaker Mountain	Emily Prichard Cary
The Compromise	Jo Maseberg

Ogden Publications wishes to acknowledge the following for their efforts in the publication of this book: Ann Crahan, Traci Smith and Diane Rader.